A FLY ON THE WALL

A FLY ON THE WALL

KALMAN STEIN

PALMETTO

PUBLISHING

Charleston, SC

www.PalmettoPublishing.com

The story, all names, characters, and incidents portrayed in this production are fictitious. No identification with actual persons (living or deceased), places, buildings, and products is intended or should be inferred.

Paperback ISBN: 9798991914420

eBook ISBN: 9798991914444

CHAPTER 1

IT WAS 3 AM on a humid summer night when Darcy was startled awake by the sound of a lamp being knocked over downstairs. In a panic she whispered to her husband, "There's someone in the house."

Sloan opened the drawer next to the bed and reached for his gun. It was not there.

"What happened to the gun?" he whispered, his anxiety rising.

"I don't know. I thought you kept it in the drawer."

"Goddamn it, Darcy. We already had a break-in; it's supposed to protect us."

"Well, I don't know, there's still someone in the house. I'm scared, please see what's going on," she plead.

Sloan crept to the top of the stairs and peered down into the darkness at the bottom. He called out, "Who's down there? I have a gun."

As he stepped onto the landing the floorboard creaked, and a shot rang out. The bang echoed through the house, and the smell of gunpowder filled the air. There was a groan and something heavy fell to the floor. At the bottom of the steps a dark figure ran out, tossed a gun into the bushes near the house, and ran off down the street. The screen door flapped in the night.

CHAPTER 2

MONTHS EARLIER on a moonlit night in November, a youthful voice answered her phone and purred in a soft Russian accent, "This is Anya."

Unknown to her and the caller, someone else was listening.

"Anya, its Armando," came the reply.

"How are you, what are you doing?"

"I'm terrible, I'm awful. I miss you so much, you were so wonderful the other night."

"You were wonderful too," she replied. "We had a lot of fun."

"All I can think about are your lips. They're so soft they make me weak."

"Armando, are you trying to come over? I can't, I have the sickness now."

"Oh no no, I was just calling to tell you how much fun it was, you are so sweet, so sexy."

"And you are so delicious…"

Sloan Malone was taking it all in on his latest electronic gadget, a cell phone hacker. It was a little box he bought from a spy equipment web site for $200 dollars, and it intercepted mobile calls up to a half mile away. He had been listening to the neighborhood for weeks, but most of what he heard was just idle chit-chat and gossip. Before he had the hacker he would listen to a police scanner for hours. He liked the excitement of the police calls, but many of them were routine and repetitive.

The hacker was better. Sloan loved sitting in the dark listening to strangers. He enjoyed lurking in the shadows, spying on intimate moments. There was a glass of Bushmills Irish Whiskey on the table, and a lit Cohiba cigar in his left hand. A small curl of smoke drifted away from the window and into the room. He had the habit of keeping the cigar band on the stogie, he twirled it while he listened. The band was distinctive, there was a silhouette of a woman's head in gold leaf above *Cohiba* with *Habana, Cuba* below. The band made the stogie feel cool on his lips. He only smoked the most expensive Cuban cigars that were still banned in the U.S.

CHAPTER 3

SLOAN WROTE A POLITICAL BLOG CALLED *THE BUZZ*
that was widely read in conservative circles. He had
been interviewed on a conservative TV network earlier that day. There was nothing more satisfying to
him than expressing his opinion on anything and
everything, and second guessing everyone. The in-
terviewer was Serena Gaulwirth, who had big hair
and big ambition. Sloan liked talking to women re-
porters, they asked interesting questions.

Serena did her homework before the interview.
She already knew he was smart, snarky, and aggres-
sive in print and on TV. Always the lone wolf and
never a team player, she learned the bumper sticker
on his car said Does Not Play Well With Others.
He was also known for using unnamed sources to
create headline accusations based on hearsay and
scraps of celebrity detritus. This made him a friend

to some and a pariah to others. He had rabid fans and armies of detractors who kept his click rates up and his compensation flowing.

When they met, she was struck by the large round-rimmed black glasses that dominated his face. She thought he wore them to impose a social barrier, more for effect than function. If the goggle-like glasses were a caricature, he was not aware.

He was also awkward looking; his short legs and barreled torso made him thick and squat. His hair was mottled with gray and receded to a widow's peak while dark bulging eyes gave him the sinister look of an insect. His lips were so thin they were barely visible, she thought his face seemed cruel even when he smiled. When they shook, she noted that his hands were fleshy and soft, as if he had never done much with them besides typing and holding menus.

Serena started with a softball question:

"Mr. Malone, you seem to be a controversial figure, why do you think that's happened?"

"Thank you, Serena, it's an interesting question. I think it's pretty simple, I speak my mind. In my view, humanity is only propelled forward by the rarefied few who possess talents and qualities beyond the average person. I expect, in fact insist, that struggling people must survive without aid. I've earned my success, and a lot of people are jealous of that. I'm also not adverse to skewering those that deserve it, so some people are frankly afraid."

"Who do you think deserves criticism, and why?" she replied with a flick of her eyelashes.

"I think of myself as a social gadfly. I abhor phonies, I like to recognize and unmask them. There is an endless supply of phonies in politics and entertainment, so I always have ready targets. It's a great business model. I grew up doing magic tricks, mostly simple hand deceptions, so I understand the mechanics of persuasion and perception. Then I explain the tricks so people can understand what they are seeing."

"Have you made any mistakes, was there ever a time when you discovered you were not correct in your judgement and regretted it later?"

"I can be savage with 'angels of mercy,' you know, the bleeding hearts that pretend to care about the poor. If poor people just cared enough, they wouldn't be poor. They'd have jobs, but they don't want that. Giving away money is just stupid. It doesn't help anyone. I have no intention of being my brother's keeper, or anyone else's, and too many charities are just scams to bilk donors and reward the staff. But no, I don't have any regrets, I stand by what I write."

CHAPTER 4

THE INTERVIEW WAS STILL ON HIS MIND when Sloan started listening from his office. It was on the third floor of his house in a suburb near Washington, DC. The houses in the development all had three bedrooms, three+ baths, and grey exteriors with white trim around the windows and doors. His yard had a small lawn with azaleas and buddleia next to the house, and day lilies around the perimeter. Sloan would have preferred an apartment in the city, but Darcy liked gardening. He did like the ease of using his car to go places, so the house was an acceptable compromise.

The neighborhood had a mixture of young families and retirees, most of whom worked for or with the federal government, many in national defense. Fairfax was a company town, and the company was Uncle Sam. Everyone knew everyone on the block, a lot of them from walking their dogs, and there were some scattered friendships, but no one got too close or nosy either. Sloan didn't have a dog, and he didn't mingle, although many of his neighbors recognized him from his television appearances.

Sloan's den was lined with bookshelves and the books were about history or politics, with a few on football. He had a few vanity pictures of himself with various Republican senators and congressmen, there was one with a Supreme Court justice and another with an ex-President. He liked the photos because they reinforced his self-importance. Scattered around the room were mementos from his travels. His favorite was a pair of Italian dueling pistols he had mounted on the wall, he loved the macho culture they represented. There was a large desk, a weathered leather sofa and coffee table, and a TV he could see from either the desk or sofa. The room smelled stale and musty from the years of cigar smoke.

Darcy had been sleeping for over an hour thanks to her nightly Xanax. The neighbors were chatting away as he turned on the hacker and started to scan. He first heard two teenage girls talking about their math test the next day; they both hated math and were going to sit near each other to share answers.

The conversation turned to the cute boy in the class and what outfits might attract his attention. This was going to go on for a long time, so Sloan hit "Scan" again.

Next, he heard a guy talking to his elderly mother, who was complaining about the staff at her nursing home and how she had to steal dinner rolls because they didn't give her any late-night snacks.

"You just eat the plain rolls Mom, nothing on them?"

"I have some jelly packets from the dining room; they make a nice little snack with the rolls."

"What else did you take from the dining room?"

"Oh, nothing…."

It was eleven pm when he hit Scan again and heard Anya and Armando chatting. Their flirting was a new experience. It stirred a subconscious urge in him that was sexual but somehow deeper, as if he were drawn to the scent of an ancient flower and its pollen seduced him into a stupor. What he loved, what thrilled him, was hearing someone else's life unfolding from the shadows. He had the safety of anonymity, in silence, with judgement. He was a creep, he knew it, and he liked it.

Sloan thought he recognized the girl's distinctive Russian accent. He had once been behind her at the check-out line in the grocery store when she was chatting with the cashier. A few weeks later he saw her go into an apartment two blocks from his house. She was a ripe little peach, small and curvy with a round face, sapphire blue eyes, and black hair curling to her shoulders. Her skin was pink and supple, her cheeks were chubby and flushed. She had luscious lips, full and sensual. Now that he was hearing her soft voice again, he thought the exotic accent made her even sexier than she looked. He had no idea who Armando was, but he was jealous.

"That's OK; I can't come over any way. I'm going to make a lot of money tonight" Armando bragged, and Sloan perked up even more. He could hear Armando was trying to impress the girl, and their chat was getting interesting.

"Wonderful, what are you doing?" she purred at the mention of money.

"I got a deal set up with this guy from DC. Rock crystal, beautiful stuff, he makes it himself. I'm just gonna flip it, nice and easy, easy peezy. And when it's done, I'm gonna take you where it's warm and wet and we'll drink margaritas. Ok with you, wanna go to somewhere warm and wet?"

"Oh, I love Las Vegas, let's go there."

"Sure honey, the desert's not wet but they got a lotta pools. Gotta go now, I'll call you later."

"Wait, what if something happens to you? Where will you be?"

"Nothing's gonna happen. I'm just meeting him behind the Pancake House, you know, where we have breakfast."

"Ok, I come looking for you with 'big dogs' if I don't hear anything."

"Ok, look for me with big dogs, I have to go, I'm gonna be late."

CHAPTER 5

SLOAN'S MIND WAS RACING, and the cigar wrapper was spinning. The first few weeks with the hacker had been fun but now he was hooked. This was something else, something so secretive his curiosity compelled him to find out what was going down at the Pancake House. He put on some jeans and a black turtleneck and ran out to his Audi. Darcy never heard him leave; she was still asleep.

His mind was a jumble of crystal meth and money and danger and warm wet Russian women. Adrenaline was making him sweaty; his body hair stiffened, and his eyes flared wide. On a whim he had decided he was going to go watch a drug deal go down. He flew out of the door and raced to his car.

There was only one Pancake House in town, and it was on First Street next to the interstate exit.

Sloan drove into the parking lot of the Holiday Inn next door and went around the back. He staked out a spot on a small rise where he could view the back-lot of the restaurant from a distance. His Audi had blackened windows, so he was not worried about being seen in the car, it blended in with the others in the lot. He lit a fresh cigar, inhaled the acrid aroma of the first whiff, cracked the window to blow out the smoke, and waited.

CHAPTER 6

AFTER HIS CALL WITH ANYA, Armando had started prepping for his evening. First, he checked his 9mm Glock and made sure the hammer was firing. An ammo clip with eight rounds was inserted, and he carefully nestled the gun in his shoulder holster. Armando got a shoe box from his closet, took out an envelope and counted the money inside. He peeled off thirty crisp hundred-dollar bills and put them in his breast pocket.

Tonight was just another night, a normal night. The weather was raw, the skies were darkening, and the air smelled like it was going to rain. The leaves were gone from the trees and a stiffening wind scattered them on the ground.

Armando was going to buy crystal meth, a favorite of his suburban customers. His source was Jersey Joe, a guy he met at the Laurel racetrack when he first moved back up north. Jersey Joe was otherwise known to his friends, families, and patients as Dr. Joseph Kamens. To them he was just a cheerful and successful endodontist from Cherry Hill.

Armando was amused by Joe. He knew Joe learned to make methedrine as a sideline during dental school. He also knew Joe had a bad gambling habit and was usually in a hole to his bookie. Joe had a signature package for his meth: he would wrap a half ounce in aluminum foil and sandwich wrap, fold a tortilla around both to make a "speed burrito," which he then wrapped in more sandwich wrap. Each burrito sold for $1,500 and he would bring two each time.

Armando drove his town car to the Pancake House and pulled into the parking lot behind it to meet Jersey Joe. They had used this spot before; it was dark and quiet at night. The lot was bordered by some trees buffering the interstate, an exit ramp led to the front of the restaurant and the Holiday Inn next door. The place could have been anywhere in America.

Within minutes, a white Chevy Corvette drove into the lot and parked to the left of the town car. Armando got out of his car, slid into the passenger side of the Corvette, and greeted the driver: "Hey Joe, How ya' doin'?

"Not bad Armando, I can't complain."

"Well don't, no one wants to hear it" Armando replied, and they both laughed. "You got any burritos for me tonight? I need some Mexican food."

"I got two with beans and cheese right here, all wrapped and ready to go. But I know you want a little taste, so here you are." Jersey Joe produced a little wooden box. A bluish powder and a small spoon were inside, and he offered the box to Armando. Armando reached over and dipped the spoon in the powder, brought it to his nose, and snorted a small amount. A little jolt started in Armando's nose, traveled into his brain, kicked his heart into high gear and spread throughout his body. He felt his joints stiffening as his fingers and toes bristled with new energy.

"That's really good Joe, might be the best you've made. Let me have those burritos."

Joe handed the Tupperware box to Armando, who opened it up and started to unwrap one of the burritos. Joe shifted in his seat and said:

"I checked the weights pretty carefully. I don't think you'll have a problem."

"Oh, I'm not worried too much about the weight," Armando replied, "I'll check it when I get home. Nothing personal, but I've been doing this a long time and it's an old habit to make sure I'm getting what I paid for," and he peeled back the first layer of wrapping."

Up until now things had seemed normal to Armando, but years of street dealing had fine-tuned his antennae for rip offs. When he started to check the burrito, Armando noticed that Joe's forehead looked flushed, and he saw Joe's left hand began to reach for something between the door and his seat. From drying lips, Joe said "Dude, it's all there. I've got to get going, just pay me and you can check it all at home. If there's a problem, you know where to find me."

"Hey Joe, like I said, it ain't personal but whatever you got to do can wait a few more minutes for three grand," and Armando continued to peel off the sandwich wrap.

In a panic, Joe pulled out a gun with his left hand and pointed it at the glovebox. "Listen Armando, there may have been a little mistake. I think one of them is a little short, but I'll make it up to you tomorrow if you just front me the money today. I know it's a lot to ask, you don't have to help, but I have a sure shot at the track tomorrow and I'm just trying to get even."

Armando bristled, "Why you punk, you pull a fucking gun on me you better fucking use it." His left hand snapped out and punched Joe hard on his cheek. Joe's head snapped back from the punch and his finger tightened on the trigger. The shot went into the dashboard and Armando reacted by flipping open the car door. He rolled on the ground, grabbed the Glock secured under his arm, and fired a shot at Joe who was frantically trying to put the Corvette into gear.

The shot skimmed over Joe's thigh and buried itself in the driver's door. Joe yelled "Oh Fuck" as he jammed the car into gear and floored the accelerator. The car peeled off, and the passenger door slammed closed as Joe wheeled around the side of the restaurant. The burritos were still in the car, and the money was still in Armando's pocket.

Armando was on the ground watching the car speed off when he heard sirens on the interstate, then saw flashing lights. He had been stopped a few times in Miami, but he had never been convicted of anything. He intended to keep his streak alive, so he scanned the lot and saw the Pancake House dumpster. He ran over, opened it, threw the gun inside, and closed it as quietly as possible. As he drove off, he figured he would wait an hour or two then retrieve it after the cops were gone.

CHAPTER 7

SLOAN WAS WATCHING when the black town car pulled into the lot behind the Pancake House and turned off its lights. More minutes went by, and a white Corvette pulled alongside the town car. Sloan quietly rolled his window down. The driver got out of the town car and into the passenger side of the Corvette. Sloan couldn't see into the 'Vet; the rear window was small, and his view was partially blocked by a streetlamp. His heart was now pounding, his ears straining to hear any sound from the silent parking lot.

As he watched, there was a sudden flash of light in the 'Vet and a loud shot. The door flew open, and a man jumped out holding a gun. He shot into the car as he rolled onto the ground. The 'Vet took off and sped around the corner of the restaurant. At almost the same time the sound of police sirens could be heard on the interstate and Sloan could see blue and red flashing lights approaching in the distance.

The man on the ground jumped up, ran to the dumpster behind the restaurant and threw the gun in. Then he raced back to the town car and drove off. The sirens and lights on the interstate flashed by, ignoring the exit ramp that led to the Pancake House.

The parking lot was now silent, the only noise was from the cars on the interstate.

After a few minutes, a couple came out of the Holiday Inn, the sound of their footsteps echoing in the lot. They got into their car and drove away. Sloan waited some more and still there was silence, as if the gunshots had vanished like smoke. Looking around, he slowly drove next to the dumpster. He got out of the car, tossed his cigar on the ground, and stubbed it out.

He opened the dumpster and sitting on top of a pile of garbage bags was a dark slick pistol. Sloan reached in and felt it, there was still a little heat coming from the barrel. He picked it up and it smelled of gun powder. He tucked it under his arm, got back in his car, and put the gun under his seat. He left the lot as quickly as possible.

Sloan's heart was pounding; his forehead and hands were sweaty and clammy. He drove a few miles to a shady spot next to the road and pulled out the gun to examine it. It was a dark gray Glock, a smooth marvel of efficiency. He was amazed by it, like a little kid on Christmas morning. His fingers tightened around the handle as he felt the heaviness of the gun in his hand. It was cold steel perfection, the simple elegance of form and function aligned. He flicked opened the ammo clip. There were seven bullets in it with room for one more. He put the clip in his pocket and the gun back under his seat. When he got home, he carefully stored both in a cloth bag under the sweaters in his closet.

CHAPTER 8

AT THREE AM ARMANDO drove into the dark parking lot and pulled up next to the dumpster. The restaurant was quiet, the only customer was a truck driver eating pancakes and bacon. Armando opened the dumpster, being careful to make as little noise as possible. He looked at the trash bags, didn't see the gun, and muttered *"what the fuck?"* to himself. He was sure he had thrown the gun right on top of the bags and they looked the same as before. He looked around the parking lot and there was nothing there.

He looked down at the ground and saw a cigar stub with a colorful wrapper in perfect condition. He picked it up and sniffed; it was still pungent, so he knew it had just been smoked. The undisturbed band shined with *"Cohiba"* in gold leaf and *"Habana, Cuba"* below. He slipped the band into his pocket and tossed the cigar back on the ground before he drove out of the lot.

On his way home he called Jersey Joe, who answered on the fourth ring.

"Hey Armando, how're you doing?" he said.

Armando growled, "How you think I'm doing asshole, you tried to kill me. You're lucky I don't come over there and rip your fucking lungs out."

"Hey man, I'm really sorry about that. It was a really dumb move; I shouldn't have done it. But I'm totally behind to my bookie and he's calling it in, so it was just a desperate move. I should have known it was never going to work, you're too smart a guy."

"Ok, punk, I get it, been there too. But you and I are done, I ain't buying shit from you. Got it?"

"I got it, thanks. I'm really sorry."

"Oh, go fuck yourself. I hope your bookie has a fun time with ya'." He punched the red Stop button on the phone in disgust. It had been a wasted night, and he almost got killed by an amateur.

CHAPTER 9

THE NEXT MORNING Sloan woke up more excited than he had been in years. As usual, he worked out for an hour, showered, and ate a light breakfast before sitting down to write. His column that day was about unfettered gun rights. He believed the Second Amendment gave all Americans the right to own almost any weapon of their choosing, and he wrote, again, how 'the libs' were intent on taking guns away from freedom loving Americans.

He had never owned a gun before this morning, his father was a math professor, not a hunter or a freedom-loving gun owner. The Glock he lifted from the dumpster was his first one. He was delighted to have it.

Late in the morning Darcy came down to get her breakfast of coffee, toast, and grapefruit. On a whim Sloan decided he would show her the gun, so he retrieved it from the closet and brought it to her glowing with man pride.

"Look what I found last night. After you went to bed I couldn't sleep, so I walked around the neighborhood. I ended up smoking a cigar on a bench at Johnson Park. You won't believe it, but I looked over from the bench and could see this black shape under the bush next to the trash can. I could tell that it was an object not a stick or anything, so I went over to see what it was."

He unwrapped the gun and held it out sideways for her to see. He added, "I decided to keep it for security, you never know these days."

Darcy let out a soft "ooh" as she first reached out to touch it, and she couldn't help flushing a little when she felt the cool metallic barrel. She blurted out "It's a friggin' gun. Are you kidding me, you actually found this under the bushes in the park? For real?"

"Yes, for real," he replied. "Beats me, but there it was, just like this."

"Is it loaded?" she asked.

"It was," he replied. "But I took out the clip. There was one bullet missing."

"So let me get this straight, you're telling me you just found this? I know you like having little secrets, if you're telling the truth this gun may have been involved in a crime. It could be important" she scolded him.

"I get it," he pushed back. "But I don't care. Maybe it was, maybe it wasn't, I'm keeping it anyway. You know what they say about 'finders' keepers,' and frankly I rather like it."

"But you've never had any interest in guns except politically, you've never hunted or camped out or anything. I doubt you know anything about them except that 'everyone should own one or two.'

She took the gun from him, and he heard a little girl sound in her voice as she explored the deadly machine.

"Well you weren't exactly Annie Oakley going to Catholic school and playing field hockey. Or maybe it was UConn where you learned all about guns between French class and happy hour."

Despite what he said, he loved the way she gripped the gun and the way she squirmed when she handed it back. These were the first things he had noticed about her in a long time. She usually wasn't interesting as far as he was concerned, but this was different, and he liked it. He started to rub her shoulders a little, but she pushed him away.

"Stop it," she protested. "I can't, I'm having lunch with one of the girls from the gym, I have a bunch of errands to run, and I haven't even showered yet." She went upstairs.

No surprise, thought Sloan, *our relationship has been deteriorating for years.* What had started as young love in college had not grown during their marriage. Once the glow of sex and romance faded, he saw her as shallow and superficial. They had come to ignore each other except for the logistics of living together. Each one was alone in their own space.

CHAPTER 10

DARCY HAD A LONG HOT SHOWER and thought about the gun, her skin glowing pinker. She rubbed herself with grapefruit body cream and her fingers drifted down and played a little. The sudden appearance of a gun had turned her on. After the shower she put on a sheer black lace bra and matching panties, jeans, and a casual top. She went downstairs and was all set to go to the grocery store, with a list in her hand. From the door she called into the other room to ask Sloan if he needed anything. Hearing no answer, she went to the car.

She drove around the corner, parked behind a small grove of trees, and changed into a tight black top she pulled out of her purse. She brushed her long blond hair, reapplied her lipstick to a darker red, and spritzed on a little Opium. She gave herself a little smile in the visor mirror before calling Kevin.

"Hey, how y'all doing?" he chirped. "You ready for a little lunch? I'm starving."

"Sure thing, I'm on the way now. It's been a very weird morning; my husband has a gun that he showed me."

"He had a gun? What kind of a gun?"

"I don't know, some kind of fancy black thing."

"Whoa, a handgun? Has he ever had one before?"

"Not that I know of, and it creeped me out. I have no idea what he's doing with it, but I don't like it, I don't trust him. He said he found it but, I think that's BS. I have no idea what's going on, but I don't like it."

"Where did he say he found it?'

"He said he found it in the park but that's all he said. Seems really fishy to me. But let's not worry about that. I'll be there in a few minutes; it will be good to see you."

"Well cool, I want see you too."

Kevin Kiner was popular with the women at the gym, he was tall and lanky, and could do all the advanced yoga positions beyond the members' abilities. Club management took a dim view of staff dating the members. It might happen, but it had the potential for unfortunate outcomes. Still, that didn't stop Darcy from chatting with him after class, there was a mutual attraction. After a few weeks, Darcy asked him out to lunch.

They decided to meet at Pete's Pitas, a modest Greek restaurant a few miles away, and way different from the chichi spots Darcy frequented with her girlfriends. They knew better than to eat near the club, an offbeat place like Pete's was unlikely to attract any attention.

They both ordered Greek salads and iced tea with lemon. They munched on the crunchy lettuce and gossiped about the women in the yoga class. Darcy teased Kevin "all the ladies like to get up front to get a better view of your downward facing dog." He blushed.

She noticed but didn't let on, her eyes were focused on his hands as he sliced up a wedge of tomato. She was fascinated with his hands; she thought they were expressive yet powerful. Kevin and Darcy were both enjoying the heady dance of light flirtation, and the giddy feeling of liking someone new and sensing the feeling is shared. Before too long the conversation turned to Sloan's gun.

"So why did your husband show you a gun? Was he threatening you?"

"No, he's too much of a wimp to ever do that. It was more like he was showing off a new toy. He's a pretty weird guy, I never know where he's coming from, he's pretty secretive. I don't know if he really found it or whatever. I don't think he would ever hurt me, that's not his thing, but I don't trust him anyway, and I don't believe he just found it in the park."

"Of course, I don't know the guy, but I do know what he writes and, to be honest, I think he sounds creepy."

"Oh, he's creepy all right, that's a good way to put it. I used to sorta like it, there's always been something dangerous about him, but not in any overt way. It's a little more subtle if you know what I mean, like he'd stab you in the back but never in the face, you'd never see him coming. I used to think it was kinda sexy when I was younger but I'm not so sure now, it makes me more nervous to be around him. I'm never really sure what he's up to."

"What do you think is sexy now?" asked Kevin in his soft Southern drawl.

"Oh, I like men who are confident, who know themselves. And, of course, men who know how to treat woman right. To be honest, Sloan pretty much ignores me these days. He just works on his column and watches football. I don't think he really pays attention to anything I do. It's like we live in two separate places, he does his thing, and I do mine."

"Sounds kind of awful, and actually kind of lonely."

"It is lonely. I feel like a flower that doesn't get watered, like I'm kind of drying up in the desert."

"That sucks, you deserve a lot of attention."

"Do you think so? That's very sweet of you to say."

"No really, you are an incredible woman, you're smart and funny and honestly, I think you're sexy."

"Wow, that's really nice to hear, I don't think I've heard that in a long time. You've made my day."

He blushed again. "That's great, happy to. So, speaking of sweets, do you want anything for dessert? I'm still pretty hungry."

"No, but you go ahead. I like to eat light for lunch."

"Oh, it doesn't matter with me. You know, I run two or three miles in the morning and lift before classes, so I really go through a lot of calories. Have to admit, I still have a sweet tooth, and that blueberry crumble looked pretty rad. Might have to have a cup of coffee with that too, will get me going for my spinning class."

"I love your spinning class; you have such great energy and the music you play really gets me pumped up."

"Are you coming to class today?"

"I wouldn't miss it, it's so much fun and I can burn off lunch too."

"Cool," he said while he flagged down the server. "Can I get a slice of the blueberry crumble, and maybe a cup a' coffee to go with it?"

She excused herself to go to the restroom while he dug into the crumble. When she got in the stall, she texted her friend Lottie, "Having lunch with Kevin, he's so sexy I can't stand it. He's eating dessert and all I can think of is that I want him to be eating me."

"LOL," came the reply from Lottie. "Maybe you can be the whipped cream."

"I'm working on it," replied Darcy, and she added a winking emoji.

Lunch ended and they gave each other a little hug in the parking lot. "See you in class," she said as she got into her car.

"Ok, great," came his reply. "I have to get back to the gym, I'll see you later."

Impulsively, Darcy decided she need something new and sexy, like a little teddy. Thinking about the lunch and the gun, she drove to the French lingerie store at the mall and picked up a black bra and matching panties. At five she went to Kevin's spinning class and acted as normal as possible while spinning like a person possessed to impress him. Afterward she waved good-bye and drove home to have dinner with Sloan.

CHAPTER 11

to his neighbors. Just after eleven he heard enough chatter and was about to put the hacker away when Armando called the Russian girl.

"Hey baby, I had an awful night last night."

"What happened? Are you ok?"

"Yeah, I'm fine but I'm really fuckin' lucky the guy's an amateur. The asshole tried to rip me off, he pulled a gun on me. Thank the fuckin lucky stars I kicked his arm in time, pulled out my gun and got a shot off. I was getting outta the car and missed him. Then there were a bunch of cop cars and sirens, and the guy drove off. I didn't know what to do, so I threw the gun into the dumpster. I went back to get it later, and it was gone. I have no idea what happened to it, but I'm really pissed off, I paid a lot for that gun, it's a really nice piece."

"Oh my God, that's awful, you poor baby. Come over and I will cheer you up."

"Oh man, that would be wonderful, I could use some. It's been a long couple days."

Hearing this, Sloan went to his closet just to make sure the gun was still there. He was nervous about what he had, and that was exciting.

CHAPTER 12

TWO NIGHTS LATER Sloan sat in his easy chair with his whiskey and cigar. He flicked on his scanner at ten, and the first voice he heard was his annoying neighbor talking to her sister in rapid Haitian French. He'd taken French for two years in high school, but she was speaking so fast and with such a heavy accent he could barely make out what she was saying. As best he could tell she was complaining about her husband staying in Haiti too long, she suspected he had a girlfriend there.

He scanned through more casual conversations in the neighborhood, then stopped at a familiar voice. It was Darcy on her cell phone, she was calling from her bathroom one floor below, and she was talking to a man. It wasn't a voice he recognized; the accent sounded southern.

"So how was your spinning class last tonight?" she cooed. "Was that annoying Maryanne there? She's gotten so full of herself now that her daughter has started modeling. I mean, she's a pretty girl but you'd think she was a movie star the way that Maryanne has been acting."

"Yeah, she was there. I don't really mind her that much, at least she keeps up and has some decent energy. It's the slackers in the back that get to me, they just kinda drag me down, know what I mean?"

"Oh yeah, especially the bald guy in the back. I think he's a lawyer or something, he's always trying to chat with me. He just sits in the back so he can look at our butts when we stand up on the pedals."

"Oh, you mean Tony? He's not a bad guy. He's actually my neighbor, lives a few doors over in the development. He gave me a really nice tip last Christmas and I love the M8 he drives. That thing is a beast."

"What kind of a car is an M8?"

"It's a Beemer, does 0 to 60 in like 3 seconds, costs like $130 grand. I'd love to have a sucker like that but it ain't happening until I get my own gym."

"You'd like to have your own gym some day? That's ambitious, I'm impressed."

"Yeah, it would be great. I'm working on it, that's why I've been taking those business classes. I want to be prepared. Of course, I'm gonna need some investors, and I've been quietly looking for spaces that might work. But it's not something that I can do soon, hell I'm still paying off my college loans."

In the darkness of his den Sloan was now at full attention. Darcy's voice had a tone he had not heard in years, she sounded younger and exuberant, with newfound energy. He leaned in as she continued.

"I really enjoyed lunch yesterday, you're such good company."

"Thanks" came the man's reply. "I enjoyed it too. You're a good listener, I really like that in a woman."

"What else do you like in a woman?"

"Well, you know, I like a woman that takes care of herself, but that's pretty obvious since I'm a trainer. But other than that, I really like a good sense of humor and someone that doesn't take herself too seriously. I think that's kinda hard to find, a lot of women are really stuck on themselves. I guess that's why I like you, you don't seem like them, you're a lot more, uh … confident. You know, more mature."

"I guess that's a compliment, but you make me sound like an old lady."

"Oh wow, that's not what I meant at all. I mean you're a babe, you make those girls look like nothing."

"You think I'm a babe? What a sweet thing to say, I haven't gotten a compliment like that in ages."

"No, seriously, you're a beautiful woman, you really take care of yourself. But you're also a lot more interesting than those girls. You've got opinions, you've seen things. I just think you're cool."

"You're really spoiling me now. I'm going to get a big head."

"I'm just being honest. I like being with you. Do you want to go out, like on a real date?"

"You mean at night?"

"Yeah, that would be really cool."

"Oh, I'd love to. What night did you have in mind?"

"I dunno, how about next Friday night? I don't have a class that night."

"That would be great, I'd love to. What time?"

"How about seven? I guess I can't pick you up, so I can meet you somewhere."

"Sure, seven would be great, and yeah, I can meet you wherever."

"Ok, cool. I'll pick out a restaurant, will let you know."

"Wonderful, I'm already looking forward to it."

"Cool, that's great. I have to go now. I'll talk to you later and let you know where."

"Ok, thanks. So good night, have a great evening."

"Bye for now," and they hung up.

Sloan was ecstatic listening to the scanner. It had never occurred to him Darcy might cheat on him, and he realized in a flash *catching her in an affair would be a great way to get rid of her, she'll lose alimony if I find her cheating. I should be jealous or angry, but I'm just not that interested in her and this could really work out well. This is great, and even better, I get to listen in as things develop.*

CHAPTER 13

AS THE WEEKS PASSED Sloan listened to more conversations, but he was now bored by the mundane chitchat of his neighbors. He heard two women exchange snarky gossip about a mutual friend and how she had too many Botox treatments and was losing the ability to move her face. He heard two teenage boys talk about their video game scores and then segue into the details of scoring some pot. Then he heard a woman talking to her elderly mother in exasperated but patient tones:

Her mother asked her, "What month is it?"

"It's November, Mom," came the reply.

"What happened to October?" asked the mother.

"It's over."

"What do you mean it's over?"

"It's long gone, it just happened, time moves on."

"What do you mean 'it's gone'?"

"For Pete's sake mom, it's almost Thanksgiving." Sloan could hear the young woman losing her patience.

"What about Labor Day?"

"I don't know what you mean Mom. Nothing happened to Labor Day. You can't lose a holiday, you can just have a sale on one," and she chuckled.

"Well, that's good, I really like Labor Day. We used to have picnics on Labor Day with Aunt Pauline and Uncle Hal. Do you remember those picnics?"

"Yes, Mom, I remember those picnics. You used to make us baskets of fried chicken with coleslaw, and we then played wiffle ball with Uncle Hal. Those are nice memories. I miss Aunt Pauline and Uncle Hal; they were really nice."

"Oh, I haven't thought about Pauline in years. She was so lovely, such a shame she went so young."

"So, Mom, have you eaten today? Did you take your meds?"

"I don't know."

"Is Minerva there?"

"I don't know," said Mom.

A woman's voice with a Caribbean accent responded, louder than Mom even though it was coming from further away.

"Yes, I'm here Miss Betty. Don't you worry, she ate a good meal, and I make sure she takes her meds every day. Don't you worry."

"Thanks, Minerva," the daughter replied, almost yelling to be sure she was heard. "Thanks very much, as always."

Sloan was shaken by the conversation, and he thought *this will be my fate someday, I'm going to get old and decrepit and die. Or, good heavens, what if I had a stroke and got locked inside my body unable to speak or communicate. I just couldn't handle that.*

He felt a wave of fear roll through his body, and shuddered. He needed some distraction, so he moved the scanner setting to Darcy's phone.

Darcy's voice rang out, she was talking to her friend Lottie. Sloan detested Lottie, he thought *she's one of those bleeding-heart liberals who just pretend to say nice things about people. She's a nasty gossip who talks about everyone behind their back, including me.*

Darcy told Lottie "Kevin and I are going on a date on Friday night to a nice restaurant."

"Oh, nice. Tell me all about it, I want to hear everything."

"We're going to Vicenza's in Old Town."

"Oh, niiice. A date. And to Vicenza's too, I love that place, it's so romantic."

"Yeah, I know. Sloan and I went there a few years ago, it's really nice, and very romantic. Of course, the romantic part was lost on Sloan, he looked at his phone half the night."

Sloan winced when he heard that.

"Kevin Kiner, that's really cool. That guy is so hot, I can barely control myself in his class. He makes me wet, and I don't mean sweating," which made them both laugh. "You are so lucky; I can't believe it. He could have any girl in the gym and he's talking to you."

"Well, I guess he likes older women."

"You still got it, girl. That's really cool."

"Thanks, I'm pretty excited about it."

"Well, you should be, it's really exciting. But listen, I have to go, Richard is yelling. He's watching a game, and the dog has to go out. I'll call you later."

"Ok, we'll talk later," Darcy replied, and they hung up.

CHAPTER 14

ON THURSDAY NIGHT AT DINNER Darcy told Sloan "I'm going out with Lottie tomorrow; we're going out for drinks and a movie."

Sloan thought *such a pretty little lie. I love knowing she's trying to fool me. And there's such irony, her lie is actually trumped by mine.*

Sloan spent Friday writing a column for *The Buzz* about the sanctity of life and the hypocrisy of libs who pretend to be religious, yet they let babies die so their mothers can continue to party. The mothers who have abortions and the doctors who perform them are criminals who should be prosecuted. 'We have to preserve the sanctity of life and be prepared to use execution to enforce it. It is maddening the same people who are willing to sacrifice children are also opposed to the death penalty, they are hypocrites.'

At six Darcy came bouncing down the stairs dressed to go out.

She told Sloan, "There's a rotisserie chicken in the kitchen and mashed potatoes from the deli in the fridge you can heat up for dinner."

She blew him an air kiss and swirled out the door saying, "I'm off to meet Lottie." Sloan ate the chicken in silence and had his first whiskey of the night while reading a book about John Adams. Afterwards he turned on a boxing match and watched for an hour before going up to his den to crank up his precious scanner and begin spying on the neighborhood.

CHAPTER 15

ACROSS TOWN AT VICENZA'S, the restaurant had the comforting aroma of fresh marinara. Kevin and Darcy settled into a cozy booth, and the waiter suggested they start with a bottle of *Barbera*. After a few sips, their nervousness wore off and the wine gave wings to their bravery. Darcy ordered cheese tortellini; Kevin opted for veal.

Kevin asked, "Do you know any of the other women that take my class with you?"

"Well, I know Lottie pretty well, we've been buddies for a long time, but I don't know many of the others very well. I do know they talk about you in the locker room." This made Kevin blush a little, which Darcy thought was cute.

"Does that bother you?" she asked.

"Oh, that's nice of you to say, I guess it never hurts when women like you. Probably helped me get the job if I'm being honest."

"I think that's very sweet, both your honesty and humility. I don't think there are a lot of guys in your position that think that way, most of them just want lots of girls around."

"Oh, girls are nice I suppose, but I prefer the company of a woman such as yourself, someone who's lived a little and is more mature."

"Are you calling me old again?" she said with a nervous giggle.

That made him nervous. "Oh no never, that's not what I meant at all," he stammered. "I meant someone with more perspective. The twentysomethings are cute, ok, but they don't know anything about life, they just want to, you know, and then there's nothing to talk about, no perspective. A woman like you has been places and understands things."

There's nothing wrong with a humble hottie, she thought, *it makes him even sexier.* She also wanted to change the subject from her age, so she asked him, "What places interest you?"

"Oh there are so many places I want to go, I'm just a hick from North Carolina and there are so many. But I guess if I had to pick one it would be New Zealand. Have you been there?"

"No, I haven't but I hear it's lovely. That's an interesting choice, why there?"

"Honestly, it was from watching the *Lord of the Rings* movies when I was a kid, I just became fascinated with the country. For such a small place it has everything, including the Māori's, who are way cool to me, especially their tats. Where would you like to go?" he asked.

Darcy replied, "I want to go to Sicily. I've been to other parts of Italy and loved all of them. I imagine that Sicily is more rural, less touristy, and even more romantic than the other sections. And I love the Sicilian concept of *omerta*, the code of silence and honor placing loyalty to the clan above all else, including the law. To me it means love and dedication to one another that is unshakable even in the face of death."

"Wow, that's really deep, I love it."

The waiter showed up and asked if they'd like dessert or more wine. They settled on shots of a strong *grappa,* and they shared a scoop of almond *gelato* with two spoons. The fragrance of flirtation wafted through their evening like the sauces graced the meal, they were satisfied now but hungry for more. They shared a warm hug outside the restaurant as they parted, and it lingered longer than friendship.

CHAPTER 16

ON SATURDAY NIGHT Sloan and Darcy had dinner together while they watched a Bond movie they had both seen before. They didn't speak much, each of them was thinking about what had happened on Friday night. At ten the movie finished, and Sloan excused himself, "I'm going up, I'm really into this book about John Adams. Did you know he actually jailed journalists that disagreed with him? He's my kind of guy."

In the office he settled down with another whiskey and lit a fresh Cohiba. He turned on the scanner, started twirling the wrapper on the cigar, and waited. Twenty minutes later his anticipation was rewarded, and Darcy's voice came over the airwaves.

"Dinner was so much fun. You are such a good listener. I'm so used to Sloan and all his nasty opinions and you're so positive."

"Darcy you can't let that stuff get you down. Yes, he is an ass, but you have to be your own person no matter what he says."

"You are so right, and it's really nice to hear. I feel like a flower in the desert that's been dry for years. All I need is a little water to bloom. He could care less what I'm doing, and honestly, I don't know if he cares about anything other than his column. He doesn't even give a crap about his readers. He just wants to spew and have somebody agree with him. Or not, he also likes it when people argue."

"Well, it's his loss, you are such an interesting person. I love spending time with you."

"I like spending time with you too. But we do have to be careful, I don't think he would like it at all. I can't imagine what he would do, especially now that he's got a gun," she said with a nervous laugh. "Of course, we've done nothing wrong, it's just how appearances are."

"I understand, the last thing I want to do is cause you a problem. Are you saying we shouldn't see each other?"

"Oh no, I'm not saying that at all. I'd love to have dinner with you again. It's just that we can't go further than that."

"Oh, that's not a problem, we're just friends, I just like being with you."

In the darkness of his den Sloan had finished his drink and was still working on his cigar, smoke curling to the rafters. *How nice that things are working out,* he thought. *These two are really playing a game with each other, it's just a matter of time until they take the next step.*

CHAPTER 17

ARMANDO STARTED VISITING LOCAL CIGAR SHOPS.
He told the shopkeepers he met a guy at a party who gave him a Cohiba Esplendido. He said he didn't get the guy's name, and the hostess didn't know who it was. "I want to thank the guy, but honestly, I just want to see if I can get a few more sticks, it was such an amazing smoke."

The shopkeepers understood, the Esplendido was a legendary cigar that was not for sale anywhere. Armando actually had his own connection for contraband Cuban cigars in Miami, he had dealt them for years as a lucrative sideline. But he hadn't sold them since he left Florida, and he wasn't a smoker.

He visited three shops, and no one had a clue. Most of them had never seen an Esplendido. The reaction was different when he got to the fourth store.

"Oh, I know a guy that smokes those," said the man working the counter. The shop was dark and narrow, and it reeked of stale cigar smoke. "He comes in here from time to time to buy a box or two of Fuentes. He likes to show me his Cohibas and brag about 'em. He's one of those guys you see on the news shows, name is Sloan Maloney. He's a decent customer but honestly, he's a weird looking guy. Kinda looks like a giant bug, and he thinks a lot of himself. But those cigars are awesome, they even smell great. I tried to buy one from him and he wouldn't do it. You're lucky he gave you one, he must really like you."

"Yeah, we hit it off pretty good," Armando replied. "It was a great party, and we were both a little drunk. I think he was showing off by giving me the stogie, but it was a nice thing to do. Anyway, thanks very much, that's what I needed," and he left the store. He went to his car and googled the name Sloan Maloney.

When Sloan Malone's picture and Wikipedia page popped up Armando realized Sloan was a semi-famous guy known for his conservative writing and TV appearances. A few more clicks and he figured out Sloan lived near his girlfriend Anya. He wondered *Could this guy have been in the back lot of the pancake house? Maybe he was just eating there, and a cigar band fell out in the parking lot. Could be that's all it was.* But years of working the streets gave him an instinctual feeling *there are no coincidences. I'm going to check out this guy's house, see what I can learn.*

Later that night he went over to Anya's apartment, and he showed her Sloan's picture. He asked if she had ever seen him.

"Yes, I do think I've seen him, but I don't know where. At a bar, or the neighborhood, I don't know. He seems familiar, but I can't place him. Why are you asking?"

"I think he might have something to do with my missing gun. I found a band from a cigar in the parking lot where I lost the gun. It was from an expensive cigar, a Cuban cigar, the kind you can't buy legally. Seems odd that it would be in the parking lot of the Pancake House. I checked with one of the local cigar stores and they knew who the guy was."

"So, you think he might have your gun?" she said.

"I don't know. It's odd. But something happened to the gun, it just didn't walk away. And it's registered to me, so if he does something with it, it could come back and bite me in the ass."

"I could bite you in the ass," she said with a sly smile. "I like cigars too."

"You do?"

"Oh yes, I like to suck on them," she said grinning, her blue eyes sparkling. "You know I like to suck on long thin things." Armando took the hint and sat down on the couch next to her. He put his arm around her shoulder and gave her a long, deep kiss.

"Maybe we should go in the other room," she suggested.

"Maybe we should," he replied as he took her hand and led her into the bedroom.

CHAPTER 18

HAVING HEARD THE FLIRTY PHONE CALL between Darcy and Kevin, Sloan knew in his gut the relationship was going to progress, cell phone conversations were never going to be enough. He liked the idea. In secret he hoped if they become lovers, it would be a great excuse to divorce Darcy. *Our relationship has been deteriorating for years, I could keep my hands clean and avoid all the emotional crap and the alimony payments.*

He figured Kevin's apartment was the logical place where they might consummate an affair. He had a flash of inspiration, and without hesitation decided *I'm going to bug Kevin's apartment.*

The idea titillated him to his core, it appealed to his voyeuristic and secretive nature, and he started to develop a plan.

It didn't take long to find a workable spy camera on-line. The cameras he found were nanny-cams disguised as everyday objects like clock radios or cell phone chargers. Those weren't going to work. He couldn't put something in an apartment he'd never seen. But one device was perfect for this application. It was a camera hidden inside a standard electric receptacle and it looked and functioned like a normal wall socket. The camera even had a strong wi-fi signal and an app. Once it was installed inside Kevin's apartment, he could receive a live picture on his cell phone. It could be wired to tap power from the receptacle, and the outlet could still be used as normal.

Sloan ordered three of them for overnight delivery. After the cameras arrived, he practiced installing them using the outlets in his office.

CHAPTER 19

SLOAN FOUND KEVIN'S LAST NAME on the gym's web site, and Kevin's address was easy to find on-line, so he decided to check it out. When he pulled into the parking lot at Kevin's development and found the address, he realized he was in luck. Kevin lived in the last house on the end of the row, he didn't have any neighbors on one side, and there was a row of thick hedges that shielded the small backyard behind the three-story townhouse.

He already knew Kevin taught a six pm spinning class on Monday nights at the gym, which was after dark during November. The following Monday morning he told Darcy "I'm going to a card game at Benny's house at six tonight. He's going to have sandwiches and snacks, so I'll just eat there."

"No worries," she said. "I'm going to spinning class, and I'll get a bite with Lottie after that."

Sloan drove to Kevin's, pulled into the farthest spot in the lot, and scanned it to be certain no one was around. Armed with a screwdriver and the cams, he went around to the back of the house and found a gray wooden fence with a chain to open the gate. He pulled it and stepped in. It was a small space, a pocket yard with a small patio and just enough room for some neglected bushes, an inexpensive chaise lounge and a small Weber grill. At the other end was a glass door, next to it was a garden gnome on a little pedestal.

He went to check the door, and it was locked. There was a floor mat by the door, and he looked under it, but there was no key. The felt around the top of the door frame, there was nothing. He glanced at the gnome next to the door and picked it up. To his surprise there was a key under it. The key opened the door, and he carefully put it back under the gnome. He stepped into the room. His heart was pumping now, this was the first time he'd ever broken into someone's home, and excitement and fear started to make his pulse race.

He was standing inside a little eating area next to the kitchen. On the other side of the kitchen was a modest living room. On one side of the living room a flat screen TV was sitting on top of a credenza. Facing it was a sofa and side chair, all of it looking like Crate and Barrel. There was a photo of a sandy white beach above the sofa, and a coffee table in front. Next to the sofa was a large fish tank with some angel fish and tetras placidly swimming around a little castle in the middle.

Next to the credenza he found the one critical thing he needed, a wall socket facing the sofa. Screwdriver in hand, it didn't take Sloan long to remove the plate over the receptacle and install the spy-cam, being careful to work around the open circuit so he didn't get shocked.

He opened the app for the spy-cam on his phone and found there was a public wi-fi source in the area. He connected to it and could now view the video feed on his phone. He screwed in the wall plate. It was identical to the one he was replacing except for a little shaded white area between the two outlets. No casual observer would ever notice it. His adrenaline was pumping, yet he was elated at how easy it had been.

Next, he went up the stairs and found Kevin's bedroom. It was a mess and had a faint odor of sweat. The bed was unmade with a rumpled comforter strewn on top, and dirty clothes were littered around the room. There was a chest of drawers across from the bed topped by a large mirror tilted so someone in bed could see their own reflection. A jumble of sneakers was piled on the floor.

Light from the parking lot filtered in through the blinds on the window. Underneath the window was what Sloan was looking for, an electric outlet with the standard white wall plate. It didn't take Sloan long to replace it with the spy-cam just as he had done in the living room, and to connect it to his phone. He was starting to feel real satisfaction at his success, and he was at the top of the stairs ready to go down when he heard the front door open, and two voices enter the living room below. He scurried back into the bedroom to listen.

"Dude, are you sure it's ok to come in here?" said a young male voice.

"Hey man, no prob," came the reply from another man. "Kevin gave me a key in case of an emergency, and he doesn't care if I borrow a few beers. I'll get some for him the next time I go to the store." Upstairs Sloan's eyes widened, as if it might help him hear better. The riskiness of his situation was now dawning on him, getting caught would be a disaster. He heard the refrigerator door open, then close.

"Ok, but it just doesn't feel right being in some guy's house," said the second voice.

"Dude, I told you it's no problem, Kevin's cool, I come over here all the time. But I kinda wonder what's upstairs, want to go up and look around?" Sloan's forehead started to sweat, and his hands got clammy. He heard a creak on the first stair below.

"Hey Henry, that's too much, man. Let's just take the six pack and go. I don't like being in this dude's house."

"You know Bobby, you really are a wimp. What's the big deal if we just look around a little? He's never gonna know."

"Well, I know but it's just not right. And what if he suddenly came home? This shit ain't right, let's just take the beers and go back to the game."

"Ok, but I swear you are a little wimp."

"Hey man, I ain't a wimp. Let's just get outta here, the half is probably over by now."

"Ok, ok, we're going." Sloan heard the front door open and close, and the house was quiet again. He let out a huge breath of air and wiped his forehead. He was sweating now, and his shirt was damp. He waited five minutes to make sure it was still qui-et and crept slowly back down the stairs. He went across the room and started to open the glass door, but in his haste, he brushed against a plant on a stand next to the door. The plant wobbled and fell over, spilling dirt on the carpet. Sloan put the plant back on the stand and scooped up the dirt as best he could, but there was still some on the floor as he slipped out the door.

CHAPTER 20

SLOAN WENT BACK THROUGH THE PATIO, opened the gate as quietly as possible, and peered around the grassy area behind the yards. No one was there so he retraced his steps back to his car.

He let out another huge breath once he was in the car. His shirt was dripping wet. He had a flood of realization *that was crazy and criminal and getting caught breaking into this guy's home could kill my career. But fuck it, that was great, I can't believe I did that, it feels fucking awesome.*

He opened his cell phone and checked the app that controlled the two spy-cams. Pictures of both the living room and bedroom came flickering up on the screen. The rooms were dark. He let out a quiet "yes" under his breath to celebrate his illicit triumph. He set the camera to motion-control so it would start taping when someone moved in the field of vision.

As he gazed at the app there was tapping on the window that startled him. He put the phone on the passenger seat with the screen side down. Standing next to his car was a middle-aged man in an all-weather jacket and baseball cap. He rolled down his window and asked the man, "Can I help you?"

"Hi there, don't mean to bother you. I'm a volunteer with the neighborhood watch. We kind of look out for each here, so I was wondering what you're doing here."

Sloan took a deep breath to gather his thoughts, and replied, "To tell you the honest truth, I'm having an affair with a married woman who lives around the corner. I was just watching a video while I'm waiting for husband to leave. Of course, I'd tell you her name, but a gentleman doesn't do that, does he?"

"No, of course not. I'm not trying to nose into anyone's business. I hope you understand, we just like to keep this a nice safe neighborhood and a couple of people have been seen around the backyards at night, so we're just being extra careful."

"No problem at all. I'm glad it's a safe neighborhood. You're doing a good thing for your neighbors."

"Oh, I'm just trying to do what I can. I'll keep making my rounds, hope you have a goodnight." He backed away from the car and walked off and around the corner.

Sloan had dodged being caught for a second time. With a sigh of relief, he drove home.

CHAPTER 21

THE NEXT DAY SLOAN BEGAN a new *Buzz* column. He decided his subject of the week would be about superior men; the ones who decide their own destinies and clear all obstacles they meet. Fate supplies strength to such men, providence gives them the ability to build buildings and the tools to move mountains. Lesser people are quacking ducks to such men, their little chirps and nibbles are impediments to real progress. Men such as Alexander the Great or Napoléon are the ones that make history, build great cities and nations, and forge new ways of thinking and being. Such men are heroes and whatever they produce is noble. They were not, nor should ever be, limited in their endeavors.

Sloan wrote 'most moral codes, even religions, are just devices invented to limit anarchy from the masses. Given the opportunity, most people would just indulge themselves and produce nothing. Controls over society such as strong police forces are necessary, and moral codes are inexpensive methods to limit the cost of such forces, so I do acknowledge their utility. Truly exceptional men must be allowed to move society forward by the power of their ideas and the force of their wills, unimpeded by lessors' constraints.' He did not write, but thought, *most men are sheep*.

Darcy came home in the late afternoon and gave him a little peck on the cheek as she breezed past. She had been to the beauty parlor, her hair was cut and colored, and she had a fresh mani-pedi. She had also stopped by Whole Foods and picked up chicken and side dishes for their dinner and fresh flowers for the table. Sloan thought she was lighter, her mood more pleasant than normal. At dinner they exchanged light chatter over the meal. He told her about the column he had just written, she went on about the wonderful spinning class she had taken the night before at the gym. He poured his second Scotch after dinner and went up to his den to review and edit the column.

CHAPTER 22

SLOAN SWITCHED ON HIS SCANNER and recognized the first voice he heard. It was the woman with the difficult mother.

"Honestly, John, I don't know what we can do about Mom. Her social security is just not enough to keep her in the house and pay Minerva too. But we both know she can't stay there without Minerva. That woman is a saint, she takes such loving care of mom, and mom would be hopeless without her."

"I know, Lucy, but there's just not that much money left. I've tried to move it around the best I can but there's only so much and we have to pay Minerva, or she'll find another job. I can't blame her; she can't work for nothing. I'm not sure we have a choice besides selling the house and renting an apartment. If we did that there would be enough to pay Minerva for another year. I just don't know what happens after that."

"Oh, that'll just kill her, she's been in that house for forty years. You know she wants to stay."

"Yeah, I know. But wishing won't make it happen. It just so sad, another five grand would make all the difference in the world, but we just don't have it."

"Well, I'm going to pray for it. You never know, a miracle might happen."

"It would be a miracle for sure."

"What about a reverse mortgage? I saw that guy with the mustache, what's-his-name from that Hawaii show, talking about how a reverse mortgage can keep old people in their homes."

"We've talked about that. Once that runs out there'd be nothing left for her to even move, we'd be stuck with no options. If we sell the house, we should have enough to get her moved and set up somewhere."

"Ok, I know. Sorry I keep going over it. It just seems so unfair; she worked her whole life and now it's come to this. And honestly, she gets worse and worse every day, She doesn't even know what month it is. I'd ask the church for help, but you know O'Connells just don't take charity, it's not who we are."

"I know, I talk to her too, it's pretty sad. But it is what it is. I don't think we have any good choices. I have a neighbor who's a real estate agent, I'm going to talk to her about putting the house up for sale."

"Ok, I know you're right John, that's the best thing. But I'm still going to pray, there's nothing else I can do."

"Ok with me, I hope it helps. God knows we could use some help."

Listening in, Sloan became agitated. He was projecting himself into the situation.

Crap, I've got no one to care for me, nothing but money. The fucking future feels fucking bleak. Retirement places are awful, I can't imagine spending all day with a bunch of decrepit old people. Just listening to these two I'm almost glad my parents died so young, at least I haven't gone through anything like this. Getting old is fucking horrible.

On a whim he looked up the name O'Connell and he found one nearby. He entered the address into Google maps and found a small single-family home two blocks away, he felt certain this is where the old lady lived.

CHAPTER 23

SLOAN RETURNED TO SCANNING. As frequencies rolled by there was more idle chatter, teens talking nonsense to each other, men talking sports, women gossiping about friends and neighbors. He heard chats about the weather, what someone did at work that day, what people ate for breakfast, lunch, and dinner. He had no idea people talked about eating so much and thought *no wonder everyone is so fat.* There were discussions about mindless television shows and movies, and clothes and cars and houses. The minutiae of day-to-day life somehow infuriated him, it did not interest him in the slightest.

One more spin and at last he heard what he was hoping for, Darcy was on the phone with her girlfriend Lottie. Even better, they were talking about Kevin.

Darcy was sighing. "I sat there staring at his arms last night. When the class really got going and we all start sweating, his arms just glistened in the lights and his biceps are just gorgeous, you can see every vein in them."

"Oh, stop Darce, you're making me sweat too," said Lottie, and they both giggled. "I might have to start taking that class."

"I know I sound like a silly girl. I haven't felt like this in a long time. I just like to be with him, he turns me on."

"Well, where do you think this is going? Are you going to see him again?"

"We didn't make any plans, but I think he'll call me, things are moving along, if you know what I mean. I don't know, I've never done anything like this before and part of it doesn't feel right. I mean Sloan and I aren't getting along very well these days. But it's not like we fight or anything, we just ignore each other, he goes his way, and I go mine. I guess that's what happens after all these years, you just grow apart. It's really pretty sad. All Sloan cares about is himself and his column, not me."

"I know what you mean. Richard and I don't do much with each other anymore, we don't even watch the same programs. He has his sports, and I have my dramas so after we eat dinner, we don't see each other until we go to bed. At least that's still good, he's great in bed and always has been. That helps a lot."

"Oh, Sloan and I barely do it anymore. God knows it used to be better, but I don't think he's interested. Makes me wonder if he's seeing someone. Wouldn't be surprised, he's so secretive."

Sloan smiled in the darkness of his den, twirling his cigar band. He realized his interest in Darcy started declining when he began visiting Miss Betty, a dominatrix he found on-line. Darcy was boring and conventional, while Betty was sexy, exciting, and dangerous. The more successful he grew, the more he wanted to be dominated. He liked giving himself over to someone else's power, to feel waves of sexual energy wash over his body. Listening to Darcy talk about Kevin also turned him on, he thrived on secrecy mixed with humiliation.

His reverie was interrupted by Lottie. "Listen, hon, I gotta go, my program's coming on," she said to Darcy.

"Oh, no problem," Darcy replied. "I've got some things I want to do. We'll talk tomorrow."

"That would be great," said Lottie. "Talk soon, love ya," and the call was over.

Sloan flipped off the scanner, took a swig of scotch and a puff of his cigar. There were a million thoughts in his head as he turned to editing the essay he had written earlier that day.

CHAPTER 24

THE NEXT DAY KEVIN CAME UP TO DARCY IN THE GYM.
Smiling, he greeted her with genuine warmth. She was dewy from a Pilates class.

"Hey Darcy, how you doing? How was the class?"

"Oh, it was great. Kirsten always has a good class, she's impressive."

"Yeah, I know she's really popular, one of these days I'm gonna have to take her class and check it out for myself." Kevin was a little stiff and awkward, he seemed to be nervous.

"Um…, uh, I was thinking, wondering, if you'd like to have dinner at my place on Friday night. You could, uh, meet my fish!"

"Wow, meet your fish. What a nice invitation. When you say 'meet' does that really mean 'eat'?" she laughed.

"Oh no, these are aquarium fish. It's sort of a hobby, I've had fish since I was a kid. Maybe around seven?"

She smiled. "I would be delighted, that's very sweet of you. Are you going to cook me a meal? That's pretty daring. I can be tough."

"Well I have to admit I'm not much of a cook, so I was planning on getting some take-out from Tara Thai, which has great food. Is take-out ok with you, do like Thai food?"

"I do like Thai food and Tara is good. I love their Shrimp Pad Thai."

"Cool, no problem."

"Sounds wonderful, I'll see you then, just text me the address." She squeezed his forearm and went into the locker room to change.

When she got home, she informed Sloan she was going to have another girl's night out on Friday. "No problem," he replied. "I'll see about playing cards that night with some of the guys."

Later that night he checked the signal from the spy-cams. Both were working fine; Kevin was not home. Sloan had no intention of going out on Friday.

CHAPTER 25

ON FRIDAY NIGHT DARCY CAME DOWN THE STAIRS
at six thirty wearing a bulky black turtle-neck sweater, black slacks, and flat black shoes. She told Sloan there was a lasagna in the oven for his dinner, she was off to "meet Lottie and a few of the girls from the gym for drinks and dinner, I won't be home late."

Sloan smirked behind the Reagan biography he was reading, and he tossed off "Ta ta, drive safely" as she whisked out of the house.

When Darcy was three blocks away, she pulled over and took off the black sweater to reveal a satin red blouse that matched her nails and lip color, and spritzed on a little *Opium*. She drove to Kevin's townhouse. When she got to his parking lot, she pulled a pair of black heels from her handbag and put in red beaded earrings that dangled under her light blond hair. She was ready for her date with Kevin, so she went up to his door and rang the bell.

"Well, here I am!" she said as the door opened.

He was wearing a crisp blue shirt untucked over a pair of dark jeans, no socks, and soft loafers. "Wow," he replied in his soft drawl. "You look great. I love that blouse on you, you look really sexy."

"Well, aren't you sweet, and you smell lovely. It's so nice to be noticed and appreciated."

"I definitely appreciate you. You look like a million bucks, and you're here, I really appreciate that too. I've got a nice meal for us, including Shrimp Pad Thai. I also made a little surprise for dessert."

"You made it? How cool. What's the surprise?" she asked.

"Well, it wouldn't be a surprise if I told you, would it?" he teased. "But I'm pretty proud of myself, so I'll tell you. I made a chocolate mousse from scratch. First time too, but it came out pretty good."

"I love chocolate mousse, it's one of my favorites. How did you know?"

"I didn't know, but that's great to hear. It's one of my favorites too. I hope it came out ok. Looks pretty good, and it tasted great," he said with obvious pride.

"I'm very impressed; and flattered that you made it. It was very sweet of you."

"It's sweet for sure, it's got a ton of sugar in it." They both laughed. "Would you like a glass of wine? I bought a nice California merlot for us."

"Oh, that would be lovely," she replied as she started to look around the room. There wasn't much in the living room besides a chair, a coffee table, a large TV, and a sofa. On the far side of the kitchen there was a small round table next to a sliding glass door. The table was set for two with cloth napkins and place mats, and there were flowers in a small pot in the center. She silently noted the effort he had made to make the place look nice and inviting.

Dominating the room was a large and colorful fish tank next to the sofa. It glowed with a soft blue light while a water pump was quietly whirring. A school of rainbow tetras were swimming around a little castle nestled among white rocks and tan gravel. Tiny bubbles were rising from its tiny chimney. A group of guppies had a small clique in the corner. Small plants swayed in the slow current.

"Oh, these are the fish," she exclaimed. "As promised, please introduce me. They're beautiful, what kind are they?"

"Tetras and guppies, actually. I had an angel fish too, but it just died, Yeah, I love them. They make great pets, easy to take care of. I think they're beautiful, their little rainbow bodies are so perfect."

"Oh, that's sweet too," she said as she reached out to take the glass of wine he offered. "You're really full of surprises, I expected more of a classic bachelor pad."

"Yeah, I guess it's pretty plain. I have a treadmill and some weights down in the basement. Other than taking care of my fish I pretty much just watch TV."

He reached out with his wine glass and they both said "Cheers!" as they chinked glasses. Each of them started to take a sip; he drank a big swig without hesitation, while she paused to smell the aroma, took a small sip, and then swirled a little in her mouth to savor the flavor.

"Oh, that's very nice," she said, "a lovely aroma and it tastes yummy. You have good taste in wine."

"Oh thanks," he replied, "but to be honest, the guy at the wine store recommended it, I really don't know that much about wine. I'm more of a beer guy."

CHAPTER 26

SLOAN TOOK OUT HIS CELL PHONE and tapped the spy-cam app. A lit stogie was in his hand and a chilled scotch was on the desk. The living room camera flicked on and there was Darcy sitting on a sofa with a glass of wine. She was talking to a guy he assumed was Kevin sitting in a chair.

Sloan had an unpleasant jolt. *Wow, he's really a stud. Tall, square jaw, thick eyebrows, definitely wife bait. And look at her, she's wearing a red blouse and not the black sweater she had one. Pretty sneaky, but she looks great, younger even.*

Sloan watched for a brief time as the couple chatted. The spy-cam did not include audio, it was mute for Sloan, so he had to guess what they were saying. Before long, Kevin put his glass on the table and got up. He sat down next to Darcy, leaned over, and kissed her. Her whole body leaned in to respond, their mutual passion spreading as the kiss continued. Each one wrapped their arms around the other, their fingers feeling smooth and strong shoulders. Sloan's eyes widened as they embraced *What the fuck? I thought this was going to be fun and now I don't know. I want to kill her and this fucking guy, this fucking sleazeball. This is not what I thought this was going to be, this is not fun. It's humiliating, and also weirdly exciting. I don't know, I think I'm going to throw up. That fucking scanner is evil, I can't look at this crap.*

They were talking again, and it was obvious they were discussing what had just happened, the reality of an affair was becoming plain to all of them. They kissed again, this time longer. When they were finished, Kevin took Darcy's hand and led her away from the camera. Sloan felt his neck muscles tighten.

CHAPTER 27

SLOAN TOOK A DRAG OF THE CIGAR and threw back a shot of scotch. He switched the app to the bedroom camera. Kevin and Darcy were now on the bed kissing. They were holding nothing back as they exploded with desire. The ferocity of their passion overwhelmed him. Sloan started to choke, and his stomach tightened like a fist. He was in his glory, his erotic and marital fantasies converging until he had seen enough. His voyeurism was now at war with his disgust. He clicked off the video feed and stared at the blank phone, his mind a jumble of conflicting thoughts.

Sloan was reeling from the reality of seeing his wife cheating on him, so he flipped on the scanner for distraction. After hearing the usual banal conversations, he paused scanning at the sudden sound of desperation.

It was a teenage girl talking to one of her friends and she was crying, hard. As best he could gather, the girl had a crush on Freddy. Some other girls saw her flirting and started teasing her on Facebook. More kids piled on. Her Facebook page was now swamped with "a bunch of garbage and lies," said the girl to her friend through tears.

The friend was trying to console her, but the bullying and embarrassment made the girl afraid to go to school. The idea of seeing Freddy was even worse now because he and everyone else knew she liked him. She was being called a slut and a skank on-line by strangers. Her friend asked, "have you talked to your mom about the bullying?" The girl just sobbed "she's really strict and would not understand. She hates my phone anyway; she'd just take away it if she knew."

The friend suggested "try talking to someone at school, like Mr. Garrison. You know, Arlene went to him when she thought about dropping out of school, and he talked her out of it, so she thought he was a cool guy. Might help, you never know."

"No," sobbed the girl. "Mr. Garrison's ok, I guess, but he'll just tell my mother. There's no way out of this, I'm just completely fucked. Freddy's never going to have anything to do with me. I'm just fucked and there isn't a damn thing I can do. I want to throw myself off a bridge, that'll serve them all right. That's what they want me to do."

"Georgia, no one wants you to do that," the friend replied. "That's crazy talk. I know you're really upset, but it's going to be ok. You'll see."

"No, it won't," said the girl again. "The entire world thinks I'm some sort of whore just because I put on a short skirt and wore makeup. You should see all the comments on my page, there are hundreds of them, and they just keep coming and coming. Like it's some kind of big joke, like *I'm* some kind of big joke. It's horrible. I'm just going to throw myself off that fucking bridge. That'll show them, it won't be so much fun then, will it? I'm just going to throw myself off the fucking bridge, that'll show the fuck-ing assholes," and she started to sob even more.

"Georgia, you can't let this get to you," said the friend. "They're all assholes, you can't give them the satisfaction. And all those people are just trolls, they don't mean a damn thing."

"But what am I supposed to do about my page? They've written all this crap; how do I get it off? Should I just close my account?"

"I think you have to block them and then report them to Facebook," said the friend.

"That would take days, and then people already know all about it. I even got teased about it by that dweeb Stevie at school. The damage is done, there's no going back. I'm fucked."

'Oh, Georgia, you just can't talk like that. I know it sucks now, but you have to just block the trolls and report them. That's the kind of thing you can talk to Mr. Garrison about, I think it's the kind of thing he can help with."

"I'm not talking to Mr. Garrison; I'm not talking to anyone. I'm just fucking done, I'm fucking screwed," she repeated. "I have to go now Annie, I can't talk about this anymore, it's just to fucking awful. I gotta go, I'll talk to you tomorrow."

"Ok, see you at school tomorrow?"

"I don't know. Yeah, I guess so, but I don't know. Maybe I'll be there, maybe not. We'll see. But I gotta go, talk later." She hung up the phone, still sobbing.

The air in Sloan's den was still, the room was silent.

Sloan was stunned by the conversation; it was so raw and real. He empathized with the pain and embarrassment he heard in the girl's voice; it felt close to how he had felt growing up. The scanner crackled again; she was calling someone else.

CHAPTER 28

A SOOTHING FEMALE VOICE ANSWERED THE PHONE: "Hello. You've called the Suicide Prevention Hotline. If you're in emotional distress or a suicidal crisis, or are concerned about someone that might be, we are here to help. If you are in the military, press one. If not, hold on and we will route you to a provider in our network near you."

There was a long pause and the sound of phone lines clicking. Another soothing female voice came on the line and said, "This is Melissa with the crisis and suicide prevention center, who am I speaking with?"

"My name is Georgia," sobbed the girl.

"Hi Georgia. How are you feeling today?" asked Melissa.

"I don't know. Everything's just so fucked up."

"Do you want to talk to me about it? Maybe I can help."

"Nobody can help, I fucked it all up," howled Georgia.

"Maybe not, but I can listen if you want to talk. That might help. You never know, it's worth a try."

"Well, there's this guy at school. I have a crush on him, and some of the kids caught us talkin' so they put all this crap on my Facebook page. There are hundreds on there, they're just awful. Now everyone's making fun of me. I can't go to school with them all staring at me."

"Oh, that's terrible. Georgia, do you live with your mom and dad?"

"I live with my mom. She's separated from my dad and anyway, he's in the army so he's away a lot of the time."

"Have you talked to your mom about this?"

"I can't talk to her about it. She's really strict, doesn't want me to have anything to do with boys. She'd ground me if she knew I'd been flirting, much less all the other stuff."

"What other stuff?"

"Well, I've kind of been fooling around with Freddy, but nobody really knows that, not even my best friend."

"Have you had sex with Freddy?" There was a long pause.

"Just once," said Georgia meekly. "No one's supposed to know about it. We just did it once and he promised to pull out before he came but then he didn't." She started sobbing again.

"Oh my, do you think you might be pregnant?"

"I don't know. Maybe. It was a couple of weeks ago and I haven't felt very good since then," she confessed. "I think I might be."

"Have you taken a test?"

"No, ma'am, no test. I guess I could, maybe I should."

"What would you do if you are pregnant?"

"I have no friggin' clue. What would I do with a kid? Hell, I'm a kid, I got no friggin' clue. I mean, I can't have a baby, what the hell would I do with a baby? But there's no friggin' way I'd have an abortion either. I don't have the money for anything like that, and my mom would fuckin' kill me. And I don't even want to think about what my dad would do, he'd just go fuckin' crazy, I think." She was crying even more now and having trouble breathing as the words came tumbling out.

"Ok, Georgia, let's try and calm down a little. I really think you should talk to your mother; you are in a tough spot and could use some help."

"I don't know what to do," she said but she could barely get the words out between sobs.

"Let's try to calm down" said Melissa in her most reassuring tone. "Maybe we can figure it out."

"Yeah, we'll just figure it out," spit Melissa. "There's no figuring this out, I'm just fucked. You know what I mean?" Suddenly the phone clicked off and there was dead silence.

Sloan was shocked by the silence, and suddenly panicked trying to figure out what to do. But there was nothing to do, no one to call. He thought, *God I hope she's calling back the hot line, I pray she is. But there's nothing I can do. I just feel so fucking helpless, and lonely.* He finished the last of his scotch and put the glass down. He was drained.

He tried to think about Darcy and Kevin, but he couldn't get Georgia out of his mind. She was so young and sad; he felt empty and powerless and panicky at the same time. He thought *that scanner is evil, there are things you shouldn't hear.*

Sloan was in his office when Darcy came home at eleven wearing the black turtleneck sweater. He didn't come out from his office but yelled down to her, "How was your evening?"

"Oh fine," she yelled back. "Nothing special, how was yours?"

"Nothing special," he replied. "Just puttering around up here. I'll be down later."

"OK," she answered. "I'm going to bed; I've had plenty to drink."

"Ok," was his final response.

The next day, and for days after, he searched the newspaper to see if there was anything, any little tidbit of information, but there was nothing. Georgia was just another teenager with a problem.

CHAPTER 29

IT WAS A RESTLESS NIGHT for Sloan as he wrestled with an intense and wild dream. In the dream he was in an old farmhouse, one he recognized but couldn't name. It was filled with boxes of all shapes and sizes, they covered the floor in the room he was in. There was a large fireplace and mantel, but no fire was burning. Two statues of dogs were on either side of the fireplace, their eyes glowed green in the dim light of the room. He was opening and closing the boxes but there was nothing inside any of them. Finally, he opened one and inside it was a small screen playing a tape of Darcy and Kevin making love. He tried to close the box, but it kept popping open, something wouldn't let it shut.

He ran out of the room and in the next room was an old woman. Her face was blurry, and she was wearing a tattered nightgown. She started yelling at him, he couldn't make out what she was saying but something was wrong, and he started to shrink. The more she talked the smaller he became. The sound of her yelling was overwhelming until she suddenly stopped, clutched her chest, and fell backwards. He panicked and rushed to her side, but she vanished into the air, and he was left staring at dust on the floor.

He woke up before dawn with a feeling of dread and a crick in his neck that made his right side achy and sore. He brewed a pot of dark coffee and watched the sun rise from the back porch, his mind tired and reeling.

Darcy came downstairs at nine. Sloan was sitting at the breakfast table reading the newspaper. She greeted him with a cheery "Good morning, how did you sleep?" as she would on any usual morning. Sloan detected an edge in her voice, a subtle shift in tone. She didn't look at him and stared out the window while she poured her juice and coffee.

"Not very well," he replied. "I had some quite vivid dreams, they didn't seem too pleasant, either." He was watching her, and he noticed she was looking away.

"What kind of dreams? What do you remember?" She was glad for the distraction.

He thought about his dreams but couldn't remember much. "There were boxes, lots and lots of boxes, cardboard boxes, and they were all empty. I don't know why but someone – I think it was an old woman – was yelling at me. About the boxes, I don't know. Then she disappeared and I woke up. That's pretty much all I can remember. Don't think I slept well; I woke up early this morning and I'm really tired now and my neck hurts. How did you sleep?"

"Me? Oh, I slept like a baby. We had quite a few drinks last night, too many, but we were drinking a nice rosé that went down easy. I always have a good time with Lottie, we laugh a lot. Slept great, feel great this morning," she said chirping a little too much. "But empty boxes, huh? I wonder what that means, I got no clue. I've never been able to figure out dreams."

"I have no idea what it means either, but it was a bad night. I watched a documentary on teen suicide, it was disturbing, almost depressing. There are some sad kids out there."

"Depressed about teen suicide? That doesn't sound like you. What about survival of the fittest and all that stuff you're always writing about? Isn't a teen suicide just one more weak person the rest of us won't have to support?"

"Maybe. You're right, but it's different with kids. We all make mistakes, we're all miserable growing up. It's awful, and there are all kinds of pressures on kids these days with social media and all that. You never know what someone can become unless they get a chance to try. I got no problem if some piece of shit down on Skid Row wants to do themselves in, we don't need more of those people. But a kid's a kid, it's just different, and it should be."

"Wow, you did have a bad night, which sounds suspiciously like empathy."

"I guess that program got to me, it was pretty emotional. I think I'll write a column about it, that would be different. You got any big plans today?"

"Oh, nothing special. Going to the gym, run a few errands, pick up something for dinner. Thanksgiving is this week; I need to start thinking about it. Any special requests? And what are you doing today?"

"Nothing special. I need to start work on a new column, haven't even thought about it until now.

Yeah, the holidays are coming, feels like summer was just yesterday. And no, no special requests, just turkey, stuffing, potatoes … you know the list."

"Ok, I'll take care of it, as always. The usual things, no problem." She went back upstairs to have her coffee in front of the TV.

The rest of the week was business as usual. Between workouts and flirting with Kevin at the gym, Darcy was busy with shopping, cooking, and talking to friends. What she talked about was Kevin. She wasn't hiding anything from them, she was extolling the new spice in her life, and her friends were enjoying the vicarious thrill of her liaison with the sexy yoga teacher.

Sloan played a round of late afternoon golf by himself. It was getting colder with the sun setting so early. He had to bundle up in layers to play, and the cold balls felt like hard rocks when he hit them. The game was not much fun now, but he persisted.

As he drove home from the golf course a black town car followed him and parked down the street from his house when he got home.

CHAPTER 30

THANKSGIVING DINNER was traditional, Darcy cooked a turkey breast with mashed potatoes and green beans, plus two bottles of Bordeaux from Sloan's modest wine collection. There was little conversation, each of them was lost in their own private thoughts. Sloan was thinking *she's such a good liar. I can't believe she's fucking this guy. I have to admit she looks great, like he's the best thing ever. But it's disgusting, and she clearly doesn't care about me. Now that I can see through her bullshit, there's even less to miss, so I'm not going to do a thing about it. I don't like her anymore, if I ever did, and this is such a useful way to get rid of her. Still, I wish I knew what I really want, I'm not sure this is it. This might be a huge mistake.*

Later that night Sloan decided to amuse himself with his scanner. As he expected, there was a lot of chatter about relatives who had just been over for holiday dinners. People seemed to enjoy gossiping about their families and how gross or inappropriate they had been. As he scanned through a swirl of conversations, he heard a familiar voice talking to one of her friends.

"It was very sad. She doesn't remember anything for five minutes. At least she still knows who John and I are, I'm grateful for that."

"How's her appetite? It's really a problem when they stop eating, happened with my Granny."

"Oh, she eats like a horse. You should see her plow through the potatoes, both the mashed *and* the sweet ones with the marshmallows on top. God knows the O'Donnell's love their potatoes, doesn't really matter what kind or what you do to them. Mashed, fried, sweet, with cheese or without, doesn't matter. She ate two full plates; God knows what Minerva will have to deal with later." They both chuckled at that.

"Well, that's a blessing, for sure. But I thought you were going to have to let Minerva go."

"We are going to let her go; we only have money for another three months. John is talking to the Hidden Valley retirement center about moving her there so we can sell the house. We've been putting off the whole thing so mom could enjoy the holidays in her house. Probably be the last time. It's not going to be fun. She's told me a million times she wants to stay in that house, and she just hates the idea of going to a home, but I don't know what else we can do."

'Oh, that's awful. There really should be a way to keep folks in their houses. But the retirement places do ok, and Hidden Valley isn't too bad. I had my aunt there for a few years before she passed. She didn't care for it; she hated the food and thought it was depressing. And she missed her garden, which had always been her pride and joy. But they took good care of her until the end, they seemed ok to me."

"Well, we're dreading have the conversation with mom, there's no good way to do it."

Sloan sat in the dark with his scotch and cigar feeling empty. He hated to hear this conversation, as it penetrated to a deep level of anxiety over his own future. There was no one who was ever going to care whether he was in a house or a home, or if he got sweet potatoes for Thanksgiving dinner. Something about this old woman and her family was troubling to his core, and it roused him to unfamiliar action.

CHAPTER 31

THE NEXT DAY WAS BLACK FRIDAY. Rather than go shopping with the masses, Sloan got up early and went to the bank. He withdrew ten $1,000 bills from his bank account, put the bills in a plain white envelope, and wrote "Happy Holidays from Santa" on it. He drove to the small house near his neighborhood and put the envelope in the mailbox marked "O'Donnell."

The act thrilled him, he loved the idea of being a secret Santa, of changing someone's life from the shadows. An unfamiliar feeling was creeping in, he was glowing with warmth on a cold and windy day. He picked up the newspaper from the lawn on his way back into the house. He went into the kitchen and made himself a turkey sandwich from last night's leftovers, sat down to eat, and opened the paper to catch up on the news.

'Cyber-bullying Claims Local Teen' read the headline in the local section of the paper. The story went on about a teenager found unresponsive, likely of suicide. The teenager's name and the cause of the death were withheld due to the age of the victim. In their grief her parents had contacted the paper hoping it would run the story. They knew about the cyber-bullying and thought it caused the teenagers' troubles. Despite their loss the parents hoped some good might come from the death of their daughter. The paper reported the teen had been the recipient of a viscous campaign on Facebook, now taken down, with hundreds of teasing and provoking comments posted to her page.

In his heart Sloan knew *this was Georgia. I am fucking devastated, crushed. I know what I heard on the scanner, there wasn't anything I could have done to prevent it. Nothing makes any sense. Even if I tried to help, I couldn't reveal I was listening, it's friggin' illegal. I had no idea who I was listening to, or what on earth I could have done to change the outcome. I know I was powerless, but somehow, I still feel guilty, like I was responsible. That's just crazy.* He was pacing around the room puffing hard on his cigar.

As he paced, he walked by an old guitar perched on a small stand. He hadn't played it for years, and it was just collecting dust. As he walked by the guitar, the D string snapped and was broken. He hadn't touched the guitar, there was no obvious reason why the string snapped at that moment. He stared at it in disbelief, curious as always to understand the logic. The guitar had been sitting on the same stand in the same place for years. The snapping made no sense, it just happened. The two events, the suicide, and the string, merged inside his mind and the more he thought about it, it became the inspiration for a new column.

The subject of the essay was about the randomness of life. He wrote "the universe is made up of molecules of energy and matter bouncing around and off each other with enormous ferocity. The randomness of bouncing molecules produces everything from stars to planets, from unfortunate accidents to lucky breaks, from teen-age angst to the sudden snapping of D strings. Any attempt to find order or logic, much less deliberate intention within randomness, is an invention of human minds needing to feel there is order, in order to feel safe. Randomness is frightening, it means anything can happen to anyone at any time. It also means no one 'up there' is looking out for anyone, we are on our own.

"It is a fact that 150 people worldwide die from falling coconuts every year, ten times more than the number killed by sharks. Despite those facts, sharks are dreaded globally, many people avoid swimming in the ocean for fear of them. Very few people avoid coconut palms. Coconut palms look lovely and benign, people associate them with warm ocean breezes, and they are an enduring symbol of the tropics. Still, consider the randomness of death by falling coconuts, it's as illogical as the moment a guitar string snaps for no apparent reason. The string does not choose the moment to snap, and the palm tree does not decide it is time to shed a coconut and kill an unlucky person walking below. There is no way to understand these facts, there is no reason why, there is no intention behind the events. The only thing to do is to accept them, the string snaps, the coconut falls, people die for no reason other than being alive.

"Accepting the reality of randomness leads to an enhanced appreciation of every moment, every second, of the life we are granted. If the universe is a random collection of colliding molecules, each of us is indeed lucky to be a collection of molecules colliding in the moment. No one knows how long their moment will last. Being human, each of us has a capacity, unique in the universe, to comprehend and understand our individual luck, as well as the randomness of our own and collective existence.

"Time is our most precious resource next to life itself, because none of us knows when a coconut will fall from the sky and end our existence. Creating a culture of life means preserving it in every form, even if objectionable or painful, from inception to death.

"Thanks in part to social media there is epidemic of teen suicides. Suicides are the ultimate denial of our luck amidst the randomness of the universe because suicide wastes the gift of life. Guitar strings all snap eventually, there is no need to pull one early and cause it to snap before its time. Life might be an illusion, a magic trick produced by a mischievous god. It is possible our perceived existence is nothing more than a fleeting moment in the mind of a formidable presence in the universe. Yet, in the absence of any true proof, all we can do is bask in the glory and magnificence of the moment, of any moment of consciousness and life."

It was dinner time when he finished the column. Darcy came home from a day of shopping, and they ate leftovers quietly. After dinner Darcy went to the bedroom to watch movies, and Sloan went to his den to watch a basketball game. He didn't feel like listening to the scanner in the evening, it now felt painful. It had been a long day of emotional swings.

CHAPTER 32

TWO NIGHTS LATER Sloan was listening on his scanner when he heard a familiar voice, but this time there was a sense of joy he had not heard previously.

"I swear it's a Christmas miracle, God has been listening, and he answered our prayers. I mean, we were days away from sending Momma to the home, we just didn't have the money to pay Minerva and keep her in the house, and out of the blue there's ten thousand dollars in the mailbox. I just can't get over it."

"Ten *thousand* dollars?! Good heavens Lucy, that's a heck of a lot of money. What do you mean 'it just showed up'?"

"Yes, just showed up out of the blue, as if God put it there. I opened the mail, and there it was, ten one-thousand-dollar bills in an envelope. Says it's from Santa. I've never even seen a thousand-dollar bill before. And honestly, I have no idea who would have done that. I mean, it's not like I run around asking people for money, you're one of the few people I confide in. You know how private we are, we don't ask for charity, we keep to ourselves."

"That's true, y'all are that way."

"I mean, it's like someone was listening, someone just heard us and then there was just this secret Santa. I tell you, it's a miracle."

Sloan was now grinning from ear to ear, the happiness almost exploding out of his chest. *I've never done anything like this, I don't even donate money to charities unless I get my name in a book or something that might increase readership. This is new and I liked it, feels kinda warm inside. I'm going to do this again, and I'm going to keep doing it until the old lady goes. Maybe someone might show me the same kindness, or maybe there is a heaven and I'm just hedging my bets. Either way doesn't matter, this is the best I've felt in years.*

CHAPTER 33

THE NEXT NIGHT Sloan was feeling so good he decided they should eat out at their favorite Chinese restaurant. He dressed in his usual uniform of black slacks, shirt, and shoes. Darcy hopped into the Audi wearing a long fashionable sweater from Eileen Fisher over slim cut jeans and heels, the scent of *Opium* following her. Sloan thought *she smells great, she's looks great, and she's in a great mood. I know it's thanks to Kevin. I wish I still made her feel that way, but it is what it is.*

Sloan drove a few miles. They were almost at the restaurant when he realized "Jeez, I left my cell phone, it's probably sitting on my desk. I feel naked without it, and we're not in a hurry, so I'm going back to get it." He turned the car around.

The house was dark when they pulled up. Sloan thought that was odd, he was sure he had left the lights on in the front hallway, as usual. He got out of the car, walked up on the porch, and started to put his key into the lock, but he fumbled a little since it was so dark on the porch. As he started to turn the key in the lock, he heard a noise in the house. There was someone running down the stairs, and he heard them run into the kitchen and out the back door. He ran back out to the car, got in, and told Darcy to call the police, someone had broken into their house.

They were terrified waiting for the police to come. Even though they heard someone run out of the back door, they were too scared to go inside. After a few minutes, the police arrived, and they all went inside. The police went through the house to make sure no one was still there. They found a small window in the back door broken; the intruder had reached through it to open the lock. Almost nothing else was disturbed in the living room or kitchen, the only sign of the intrusion was in the bedroom where the drawers of the nightstands and the dresser were pulled out. It was as if the intruder was looking for something specific and had been interrupted by the arrival of Sloan at the front door. It did not appear anything had been stolen. The police assured Sloan and Darcy they would cruise past the house for the rest of the evening and the next few nights, and they left.

CHAPTER 34

ARMANDO HAD BEEN OBSERVING THE HOUSE ever since he figured Sloan might have his gun. He had patiently watched movements in and out of the house through the blackened windows of his town car parked down the street. After he saw the couple leave for the evening, he went to the back door, covered the small windowpane with the side of his jacket, and punched it out. Armando reached in, opened the lock, and slipped into the kitchen.

Armando wasn't there to burgle the house, all he wanted was to get his gun back. For safety people usually keep guns next to their beds or in their dressers or closets, so he crept up the darkened stairs and found the master bedroom.

He was rummaging through the bedside table when the car drove up, followed by footsteps on the path, then onto the porch. There was barely enough time to escape, and as someone started to open the front door, he ran out of the house through the back door and into the neighbor's yard before circling all the way back to his car. By the time the police arrived Armando was gone, unnoticed.

As a result of the break-in, Sloan moved the gun from under the sweaters in his closet to his bedside table in case the intruder came back. It had been a scary incident and now they felt they needed security. They had no idea why someone had broken into their house, neither of them connected the incident to the gun Sloan had found.

CHAPTER 35

DESPITE THE BREAK-IN, Darcy was riding high on a cloud of elation when she had lunch with Lottie a few days later. "I swear Lottie, I feel like I've been released from a dreary and depressing life. I'm just exhilarated being with Kevin. And satisfied, if you know what I mean," and they chuckled a little. "There must be something about forbidden fruit that makes it more exciting and erotic. Of course, I've always had a little on the side, and I don't care if Sloan has too, although I doubt it. But Kevin is such a gorgeous and virile man, his body is amazing. And I know all the women at the gym want him, so it's really flattering and thrilling. I don't know, but this relationship makes me feel younger and more attractive than I have in years."

"Count yourself lucky honey, but be real damn careful to hide it. I'd hate to think what Sloan would do if he found out. And now that he's got a gun, who knows what could happen?"

"Oh Lottie, Sloan is harmless, he wouldn't hurt a fly."

"Maybe so, just please be careful, these things can blow up fast."

CHAPTER 36

KEVIN WAS HAVING A FEW BEERS with Tony, a student in Kevin's spinning class and also a neighbor in his development. Three beers loosened Kevin's lips.

"I know I'm playing with fire by doing it with a married woman, but man, I love the hunt and chase of seduction. To me, it's another notch for my crotch, and honestly, it's one of the things I really like about working at the gym and being a trainer."

Tony was tipsy too. "I don't doubt it dude, some of those ladies are smoking hot, and you can't help it if they come on to you. After all, the gym is literally a place to get physical and look better, so there's always going to be something simmering under the surface."

"Dude, I loved it when they find an excuse to touch me, I totally get what's going on. It's cool. Makes me feel like I'm back in high school. Did

I ever tell you I was a running back on my high school football team? I was good man; I made the second team all-state.

"Yeah, you told me. It's awesome man, and I can totally see you were a stud."

"Yeah, well that was a long time ago and frankly it's been tough since then. Don't get me wrong, I like training, but it's hard to get ahead on what we make."

"I can see that, can't be easy, even with the easy pussy."

"Yeah, I'm hoping one of the ladies comes through."

"What do you mean 'one of them'? Are you dating more than one?"

"Oh yeah man, I'm juggling three of them. It ain't easy, but it's also kinda fun, and I have to admit I enjoy the game.

"Dude, I can't believe you can do that. I've got a girlfriend, and one is plenty. I can't imagine three at a time. You are a brave man, I'm in awe."

"To me, none of the relationships are serious, they're just harmless fun and games. I'm always polite and respectful of women, and I never make promises I can't keep, so I don't think it's all that wrong."

"Who are they, how do you keep them straight?"

"Well one of them is a trainer, the other two are members. Two of them are just young things, nothing serious, just great sex. But the married one is older and a serious babe, I think I really like her. She's not like the others, they are girls and she's a real woman. I don't know, I like to talk to her so it's deeper than the others. Might be the best I've had, at least it feels that way."

"That sounds pretty serious."

"Maybe it is, maybe it is…"

CHAPTER 37

DARCY AND KEVIN SOON SETTLED INTO a regular schedule of Friday night rendezvous. Darcy was able to position Fridays with Sloan as a regular girl's night out and she co-opted Lottie into supplying cover for her deception. Kevin taught a popular spinning class at five pm on Fridays that conveniently left the rest of the night available. Darcy would show up at seven pm ready for fun and games, her *Opium* perfume wafting into the townhouse. She liked wearing enticing lingerie for Kevin and assembled an impressive collection that allowed her to show up every week with something he had not seen before, and they both enjoyed a little modeling session with that week's choice. One week was a white bustier, the next was a turquoise teddy, then a black bra set with a garter and stockings would follow. He found the lingerie show to be arousing and looked forward to it. She loved the attention and the obvious enhancement of his pleasure.

For the first few weeks Sloan switched on the cell phone around seven thirty, often in time to see the lingerie show. Viewing aroused him, but it was a mixed experience of humiliation and arousal, like visiting his dominatrix. He loathed the experience and loathed himself for doing it. He detested being cheated on and the stinging sensation it created.

In addition to their meetings, the lovers continued to talk on their phones at night, and Sloan was often also privy to those conversations. Their usual conversations were about their day, sprinkled with gossip about the gym members or staff.

Over the months of their meetings new sensations had started within Kevin, a deepening of his feeling of affection for Darcy. One night he was drinking at Tony's townhouse, and he couldn't restrain himself.

"Dude, I'm telling you, she's not like the others. She's thoughtful and smart, and she really understands me. I mean, she makes me laugh. She even laughs at my stupid corny jokes. I don't think I make anyone else laugh as much her."

"Yeah, but how's the sex?" Tony was joking, but Kevin was serious.

"The sex is terrific, but I actually enjoy our conversations as much or more. And I really like the quiet moments, just maybe hugging or lying next to her."

"This is sounding pretty serious."

"I dunno Tony. Maybe my looks were a barrier with other women, like they wanted me for what I looked like, not who I am. Darcy likes me, she's interested in what I'm thinking about and dreaming. It's pretty cool."

"Sounds cool, you're a lucky guy. But she's married, isn't that a problem?"

"So far, it hasn't been, but you're right. I did stop seeing the other woman; once this got serious, I just wanted to focus on Darcy and no one else."

"Well good luck dude, fucking a married lady can be tricky, or so I'm told."

CHAPTER 38

SLOAN BECAME BORED with their chats. He wasn't interested in much about either one and thought they were both dull and not smart. As the affair progressed, he often changed the scanner to find something different. He also stopped viewing the video footage. He had seen and recorded enough and watching them together upset him.

Their intimacy threatened him because it revealed his inability to connect with anyone on a deeper level. What he saw in them struck the core of his isolation and insecurity, and he started to hate Kevin for reaching a place in his wife where he could never travel. Their increasing connection created a wound in him deeper than their adultery.

Still, Sloan listened, and one night the conversation took on a surprising twist.

"I can't keep doing this Kevin, I'm crazy about you and I want to see you more. Sloan just gets creepier by the day. He locks himself in his office every night and I never know what he's doing. He just ignores me except every now and then I catch him looking at me with the creepiest expression. I really can't tell what he's thinking but I get a horrible vibe."

"Oh, who knows with him, he's a major weirdo, that's for sure."

"I want to leave him. I want to go away and be with you."

"Darcy we can't do that. You know I don't make a lot of money, and if you leave Sloan, he'll make sure you get nothing. He's mean enough, that's for sure."

"Oh, I'd get something, we have a pre-nuptial agreement, and I'd get some alimony, I think it's a few thousand a month. I just wish I had all his fucking money and not him." She laughed. "If we were lucky, he'd shoot himself with that gun and save us all a lot of grief. I wish he were dead."

Kevin heard her and said, "You're right, life would be perfect if we had Sloan's money, and he was gone. If I just took that gun and shot the motherfucker that would solve it all." He was now staring at his fish tank, "Big fish eat smaller fish, it's just the way things are in nature, the strong eat the weak."

"But I've never done anything like that. I'm not a criminal, I'm not mean or vicious like some guys. But I am competitive, and deep inside I am just tired of having so little. I know I look ok, and I can do yoga positions other guys can't dream of, but I'm really tired of having no money. Hell, I've got nothing except this stupid fish tank. I see the cars the members drive; I know the houses they live in. Frankly, I haven't felt really good about myself since high school football. But goddamn, I love you Darcy, your happiness is what's important now. This is a way to even the score, to get back on top, to feel like a hero again."

He stopped and paused, "You know, we could make that happen."

"What do you mean 'we could make that happen'?"

"Well, what if something did happen to him? Wouldn't we be better off? It's not like you really love the guy, you don't have anything nice to say about him and he totally creeps you out."

"I know, that's all true, but that's a long way from making something happen to him," she replied. "Yeah, things would be better if he just went away, if he just disappeared, but I don't know how we could do that."

"Well, what if there was another break-in at your house, and he got shot? No one knows about that gun, it's the perfect weapon. You get the gun, then I break into the house to make it look like a robbery. All I have to do is pretend to be a burglar. You hear a noise, send Sloan downstairs to check it out, and I shoot him. Sloan's dead, and the 'burglar' runs off. Who's to say that didn't happen if it looks right? I drive somewhere, throw the gun away. Even if the gun gets found, it belongs to someone else, there's nothing to connect it to either one of us. It's just a burglary gone bad, happens all the time."

Back in his dark office Sloan sat up straight in his chair and was now listening with intense focus. He was astonished by what he was hearing, but he also found it to be strange and exciting, and a sudden thought popped into his mind. *Why not let them try to kill me and catch them in the act? It would prove Darcy's infidelity and void the pre-nup.*

Would serve them right, including this asshole that's fucking my wife. What a wonderful way to end this fucking marriage. What a great illusion. He kept listening with keen anticipation to see where they were going with this.

"Gosh, I don't know," said Darcy. "Lord knows I'm tired of him and this awful marriage, but I don't know that I really want to see him dead, much less be part of killing someone. Seems awfully extreme."

"Hey," Kevin replied. "Has he ever done anything for anyone except himself? You read his columns. You know where he's at. He's always about how the strong survive, the weak die, it's a dog-eat-dog world. Every man for himself. He doesn't give a shit about anyone, including you."

"That is true. He's a pretty nasty guy, and at this point I don't think he cares much about me or what happens to me. And honestly, the feeling is mutual, I don't really care what happens to him either."

"So, let's do it, let's get this guy. Absolutely no one will miss him, including you."

"That's true, you make a lot of sense. But are you really willing to do this, to pull the trigger and actually kill him? I know it looks easy in the movies, but this is not the movies, its real life, and killing someone is for real."

"I think I could do it. I do. Look, I grew up hunting in Carolina. I've been around guns and rifles my whole life. I know which end the bullets come out. I've killed lots of squirrels and rabbits and deer, it's not that big a deal once you get used to it. You just pull the trigger and boom it's dead. And it's not like we'd have to deal with the body, we just let the cops come and they'll take care of it. And then we can be together, just like we talked about, which would be great."

"Oh, I want to be with you too," she cooed. "You make me feel great, there's nothing I want more than to be with you, I love you."

"I love you too," he replied.

Sloan was sitting alone in the dark listening, his cigar band twirling. His forehead hurt and his cheeks were burning with rage. *They'll pay for this. I know all about tricks and illusions, it's what they do in politics every day. This will be the ultimate trick to play, a great illusion at their expense. I'll play their game and beat them with it.*

Sloan started waiting each night for their chats. He was hoping to get more details as their plans evolved. They agreed to only talk about the plan when they were together, but there were enough references that Sloan had a solid notion of what they were plotting. He was on alert for a midnight break in.

CHAPTER 39

THE LOVERS DISCUSSED THE PLAN at length over the next few weeks, never wavering from the basic outline. More than anything the discussion helped to firm their resolve, both in each other as well as their intention to remove Sloan. As they moved down the path towards full acceptance, they had a flush of power, of taking control. Darcy felt the giddy anticipation of turning oppression into triumph, of striking a blow for her self-worth. Kevin felt like this was going to be the most worthwhile thing he had ever considered, as if he were rescuing the fair damsel from the dark lord of her despair. It was his chance to be a hero, to become something he could never be in his normal life.

CHAPTER 40

IT WAS A MUGGY DAY IN LATE JULY. Sloan was out of the house when Darcy slid open the drawer of the bedside table. She gently wrapped a hand towel around the gun and put it in a tote. She drove to Kevin's townhouse and gave it to him. Kevin put on some rubber gloves and checked the Glock. He confirmed the safety was on, then pulled back the extractor and confirmed there was a round in the barrel. The magazine clip was missing two rounds. Since one was in the chamber, Kevin wondered if the missing round had been fired. He put the gun back in the tote along with the clip and placed it near the front door.

Kevin spent the rest of the day pacing back and forth, tapping his pen on the table, and fidgeting in his chair, crackling with nervous energy. He thought *Darcy was right, this isn't like shooting a deer or a squirrel. I'm going to try and kill someone, a living breathing person. Yeah, he's a jerk, but...?*

I have to think about Darcy. Darcy makes me feel great, I really do love her, but I hate being the third wheel. Once Sloan is out of the way things will be great. We do this and we won't have to slip around anymore. No more being so careful about never calling her, just waiting for her to call. I hate waiting for her to call. No more hiding from the rest of the world. I can do this. I can be a hero again.

CHAPTER 41

SLOAN WASN'T SURE if this was going to be the night when he ran a few errands that day. *I hope this happens tonight, I'm sick of listening to that friggin' scanner. Most of the conversations are so banal and boring. I hear the Russian girl talking to another woman in Russian, but that's no fun. It sounds interesting somehow, but I have no idea what they're saying. I only heard her talk to the drug guy once more, just to come over to her house. I bet he's being a lot more careful since he lost his gun, but who knows?*

But yeah, I look at that scanner now and I think it's evil. I know I wouldn't want someone listening to me, that's for sure. No, this thing is evil, it's forbidden fruit just sitting there to tempt me. I'm going to get rid of it when this thing is over.

Darcy was acting odd and avoided him for most of the day, so his suspicions were aroused. When he came home in the afternoon he peeked to see if the gun was still in the drawer of the bedside table. As he had sensed, it was no longer there, so he felt certain 'the robbery' was going to happen very soon, if not later that night.

CHAPTER 42

A LIGHT FOG WAS MISTING in the moonlight. The humidity felt like a damp glove, and a perfume of magnolia and honeysuckle wafted in the air. Buzzing insects pierced the dark.

Sloan and Darcy were lying next to each other in bed. Each one was wide awake but pretending to be sleeping. Each one was lost in anticipation the night would bring relief from the other, from the marriage neither one wanted any longer.

Sloan was thinking *I'll go to Vegas for a week, drop a few bets, find a babe or two, maybe a hooker. I don't know. I hate being a fucking cuckold watching this motherfucker screw my wife. And I hate seeing her glow with this fucking affair, like she used to glow with me. I miss that, I really do, but what the fuck am I going to do now? These fucking people are trying to kill me. I mean, I hate this dude, whatever happens to him*

I don't give a shit. But Darcy's something else, I really miss her, I do, but she's trying to kill me for real. Ahh, I can't wait to get rid of these two idiots.

Darcy was thinking about her freedom. *I'm going to have my lover. I'm going to be great to get rid of that asshole and live for a change. We'll travel, live somewhere like France, go on a cruise, who knows what? All I know is it will be better without Sloan. He's such a creep. The world is going to be ours as soon as Sloan is gone.* She lay awake for several hours but eventually fell into a fitful sleep.

CHAPTER 43

KEVIN PACED BACK AND FORTH ALL NIGHT. *I love Darcy, she's a fantastic woman, so great in bed, so sexy and bad. I know she's my soulmate. But this is murder, fucking murder.*

His mind drifted between thinking about Darcy, to Sloan, to the gun, back to Darcy, and over again. The clock said one, then two, as the night crawled by. At three Kevin put on black pants, a tee shirt, and black surgical gloves. He pulled the gun out from the bag and unwrapped it. He inserted the magazine clip, checked to make sure it was still loaded, and the safety was on, and put it back in the bag. He took off the gloves and put them in the bag along with a ski mask.

Kevin put the gun under the car seat and drove to Darcy and Sloan's house, parking in front to make a quick getaway. He covered his face with the mask and put the gloves on, then went to the back door of the house and knocked out the same small pane of glass the burglar had broken. He didn't cover the glass to make sure the sound could be heard inside the house. Creeping into the living room, Kevin knocked over a lamp and went to the bottom of the stairs to wait.

Upstairs, Darcy heard the lamp fall, and whispered to Sloan, "there's someone downstairs, I think there's a burglar."

Sloan quietly said, "I'll check, no problem," and he opened the drawer to reach for the gun.

"What happened to the gun?" he whispered to Darcy in the dark.

"I don't know," she replied. "I thought you kept it in the drawer."

"God damn it Darcy," he replied knowing full well they were deceiving each other. "We already had a break-in; it was supposed to protect us."

"Well, I don't know, but there's still someone in the house. I'm scared, please see what's going on." She sounded authentic, her nervous anticipation was close to what she would have sounded like if there was an actual burglar and not Kevin waiting below.

Sloan went to the top of the stairs. Peering down he could see the outline of someone waiting for him in the darkness at the bottom. He stepped onto the top stair knowing it had squeaked ever since they bought the house, and he called out, "Who's down there? I have a gun."

As he stepped down a loud creak groaned from the step. He dropped quickly just as a shot rang out. The sound echoed in the house and the smell of gunpowder hit his nostrils. He had a small moment of elation, *he missed!*

Behind him he heard a groan, and something fell. At the bottom of the steps below he saw the shadow of a dark figure run out of the door. He turned around to see Darcy slumped behind him on the floor, blood running from her chest. She had slipped out of the bedroom hoping to see his last moment, she never expected he would duck at the last second.

Sloan let out a gasp and cried "No, No, *No!*" This was not what he expected; it was not what he wanted. He suddenly felt utter despair. She looked up at him with shock in her eyes and as he bent over her, she tried to speak but could not. Her eyes rolled back, and her body went limp on the floor, she was dead.

"Oh no, no, no," pleaded Sloan and he started to panic. He ran back into the bedroom and called 911 in a panic. As they answered he frantically pleaded into the phone, "My wife's been shot. We had a burglar, and I don't know what happened, but she's been shot. Please send someone, please, I think she's dying."

The dispatcher on the phone was calm and asked, "What's your address, sir? Is the burglar still in the house?"

"456 Ames Way. He's not here, he ran off. Please send someone as fast as you can.

"We're on the way, sir. Is your wife responsive?"

"No, she's not moving, she's been shot in the chest. Please send someone fast."

"They're on the way sir, be there in a minute."

Time seemed to slow down for Sloan, as if in a film. Blood was all over the landing. He lifted her head up to see if there was anything, but she was lifeless. Sloan started weeping in heaving waves of panic and sorrow. He knew he had lost something he loved, truly loved, even if he had not felt the same way just moments before.

CHAPTER 44

THE NEXT FEW HOURS WERE SPENT IN A BLUR OF medics and the ambulance, the flashing lights on the houses, the neighbors gathered around the front lawn. The EMTs carried Darcy outside. One of the policemen came over and spoke to Sloan while he sat on the open back of an SUV sipping weak coffee.

"Good evening Mr. Malone, I'm Detective Perkins with the Fairfax County Sheriff's Department. I'm very sorry for your loss, I take it that was your wife?"

"Thanks…I guess. Yes, Darcy was my wife."

"Well, again, I'm very sorry, but I have to ask you a few questions, this won't take long. Mind telling me what happened here?"

"Well, we had a burglar. It's the second time for this guy, it happened a few months ago. Anyway, I'm a lot heavier sleeper than Darcy and when I woke up, she was at the top of the stairs, and she said, "Who's there? I've got a gun," and the next thing I know there's a blast and she fell over, and that's all I know except there's a ton of blood all over the floor, and she's dead. She was alive a half hour ago and now she's dead. I really can't believe it."

"I know Mr. Malone, it's a lot, I'm very sorry. I just have a few quick questions. So, where were you standing when she was shot?"

"I was in the bedroom looking at her at the top of the stairs."

"And the shot came from where?"

"From downstairs."

"Did you see anyone?"

"No, there's a flash and a bang and Darcy falling, that's all I know."

"Did you hear anyone?"

"Not that I can recall, but all I could think of was Darcy. And the shot was loud, I'm not sure I heard much else…. No, wait. Now that I think about it, I did hear someone go out the back door. I heard the screen door slam shut. But that's it, that's all I got."

"Thank you, Mr. Malone, you've been really helpful, I won't trouble you anymore tonight."

"No problem, Detective, I want to catch whoever is responsible for this."

"I can appreciate that, thanks. There is one more thing. I need her cell phone, just for a few days?"

"Her cell phone? Why do you need that?"

"Well, it's standard procedure when someone has been shot. We always look at the deceased's phone."

"Ok," said Sloan. "She probably left it on the bedside table."

"Thanks, what's the access code?" asked the detective.

"It's 4, 5, 6, 7," said Sloan. "Not too original, she hated to remember all these numbers just to make a call."

"Thanks again, Mr. Malone. And I'm sorry to tell you, but there's one last thing: this is a crime scene, so you can't sleep here for the next few nights. I know that's a problem, we'll try to get you back in after a day or so."

"Wait a minute, I have to do what? And for how long? This is my home. I can't just move out."

"Sir, I'm not asking you to move out, you just need to spend a few nights with a friend or at a hotel. We need some time to figure out what happened here. We all want to find whoever did this, and this is what I have to do to figure that out. I'm sorry, it's just what is."

Detective Perkins went inside and packed up clothes and toiletries for Sloan. There was nowhere else to go, so Sloan went to the Holiday Inn and checked in. The sun was rising by the time he got into the room. The Pancake House was next door, with the parking lot behind it. Sloan looked out and thought *what irony, that's where this all started.* He pulled the curtains tight and crawled into the bed, feeling some small comfort from the crisp cool sheets.

He fell into a deep sleep and dreamt he was some sort of creature. It seemed like he was a cat. The perspective was a few inches off the ground, and inside a kitchen. There was plenty of food around, cabinets full of it, but he was not able to open the doors and cabinets. All he could do was paw at them. He started to meow. He wasn't sure who, someone put food in a bowl. He was happy now and purring.

CHAPTER 45

IN THE DARK Kevin never saw Sloan duck. He heard the groan as the bullet hit Darcy, and assumed it was Sloan. Kevin was in a hurry now, the time to get out of the house was ticking fast. He went out the back door and tossed the gun into the bushes, as they planned. Ran around the house, jumped into his car, and drove off. He was certain he heard a groan after the shot, but the gun was much louder than he expected. As the world grew silent, he could hear the blood pumping inside his head.

He drove ten miles straight out of town, pulled into a gas station and up to a pump. He got out, slid his credit card into the reader and inserted the nozzle of the pump into his gas tank. As the tank was filling, Kevin slipped the gloves out of his pocket and put them into the trash can next to the pump.

He drove home, went inside, and burst into tears when the door closed. Kevin couldn't remember the last time he cried and now he sat sobbing on the sofa, overwhelmed with the guilt of killing another person. This was not like shooting squirrels, this was a human being. He had convinced himself he hated Sloan, a man he never met. Now he was unsure of himself and his actions, killing this man seemed senseless. Kevin stopped crying, and his hearing started to return, but he stayed keyed up and agitated from all the adrenaline.

Kevin and Darcy had agreed they would not call each other after the burglary. To be certain they had concealed their plan, it was important not to communicate too soon. But Kevin was now experiencing awful emotions he had not predicted.

God damn it, I can't calm down, I'm full of nerves. I really need to talk to Darcy. We didn't think this through very well, she's the one person that can make this go away, and I can't call.

I think the plan worked, I think I hit Sloan and hopefully, I killed him. It would be the worst thing if I just hurt him and didn't kill him. Anything less than a kill would be awful; Sloan would still be around but injured and angrier than ever. Fuck man, I thought I saw a body slump over, I hope to hell it was a kill. The doorbell rang and, in his panic, assumed it was Darcy. He jumped up and opened the door. Standing in the frame was a large swarthy man he had never seen in his life.

CHAPTER 46

THE MAN WAS DRESSED NEATLY, he had on a purple tie over a pale blue shirt with a black jacket. The stranger felt menacing, so all Kevin could think to ask was "Can I help you?" The man barged past Kevin into the room.

"Yeah, you can help me. What exactly did you pull down there tonight?" said Armando. He was calm and very deliberate. "I saw you going into the house and leave the house, so what were you up to?"

Kevin wasn't connecting what he was being asked, his mind was spinning in six directions. "What house?" he asked in confusion.

"Don't get cute with me," Armando replied. "You know what house, the Malone house. I've been staking out the place, I had a bad feeling about you people. I saw you park in front and run around the back, and I got your tag number. Then I heard a shot, and the next thing I know you come out like a bat outta hell, jump into your car, drive off. So, I ran an owner check to get your address and I've been waiting for you to come home. What were you shooting, and where's the fucking gun? I ain't taking a rap for whatever you did."

Kevin flinched at the mention of the gun, Armando noticed at once.

"So you had a gun, didn't you? Where did you get it? Was it from that fuck Malone?" accused Armando.

"I don't know what you're talking about, I don't know anything about a gun," pleaded Kevin. "I'm having an affair with the lady in the house, and I thought we were meeting, but I saw her husband was there, so I ran off. I don't know anything about a Glock."

"A Glock?" repeated Armando. "I didn't say anything about a Glock. So, you do know about the gun. Where is it? It's mine and I want it back."

"That was your gun?"

"Where's my fucking gun?" bellowed Armando. "No one fucking rips me off." He took a step towards Kevin and shoved him in the chest hard. Kevin staggered a little, but his adrenaline kicked into high, and he took a swing at Armando. Armando ducked the punch and responded with a punch aiming to hit Kevin square on the jaw. Kevin was much quicker than Armando expected, and he stepped back away from the punch. He tripped on edge of the rug, staggered, and fell over backward. The back of his head hit the corner of the glass coffee table on the way down and he collapsed on the floor as blood came gushing onto the carpet.

Armando took one look at Kevin, let out a soft "oh, crap" below his breath, and went straight to his car thinking *I'm not getting that fucking gun back.*

CHAPTER 47

THE NEXT MORNING Detective Perkins found the gun in the bushes next to the Malone house. The gun was registered to Armando Goya, so Perkins and Officer Elmont went to Armando's house to ask about it. Armando told the officers the gun had been stolen from the glove compartment of his town car a few months ago, but he hadn't reported it. The detectives showed him Darcy Malone's picture, but he told them he couldn't identify her, had never met her, didn't know anyone with her name, and had no connection to her. Armando also told the officer he was with Anya all night.

The officers went to Anya's apartment to check out the alibi. She confirmed that she and Armando were together all night. She also confirmed that Armando's gun had been missing for many months, but she didn't know how he had lost it.

No other clues jumped out at the police. There was broken glass in the kitchen from the back door, and blood on the floor near the corpse, but nothing else looked unusual or out of place.

CHAPTER 48

SLOAN WOKE UP in a state of exhaustion and confusion. Reality came flooding back when the phone started ringing and he remembered that he was at the Holiday Inn. Detective Perkins was calling, he asked Sloan "please come by the police station and answer a few questions about Darcy's death when you feel you can manage it."

Sloan was overwrought. Darcy's death had hit him with more power than he ever considered possible before. *Darcy wasn't supposed to die, that wasn't the plan. I didn't kill her, but I feel like I did. I could have stopped it, and I didn't. I'm responsible. And now I miss her. She's the only person who can make me feel better, and she's gone. I even miss her narcissism and her vacuity. Now it's all just a vacuum, a void. It wasn't there before and now it just feels bottomless.*

And it all started with that scanner, that stupid scanner. That thing is evil, and I'm evil for using it. No one needs to be a fly on the wall, no one should be. People deserve more respect.

CHAPTER 49

AT THE POLICE STATION, Detective Perkins opened Darcy's phone and started going over the calls on it. The last one was to Kevin Kiner from early in the evening, and he saw Kiner was a frequent caller to the phone. Perkins called the number, no one answered. He looked up the address for Kiner. It was just a few miles away, so he decided to go over and check it out.

The address was a townhouse, the last unit at the end of the development. The detective knocked on the door, but no one answered. There was a guy walking by so Perkins asked if he knew the guy that lives there.

"Yeah, sure," answered the guy. "I know him a little. Name's Kevin Kiner, works at Donatta's gym. Everything ok?"

"Is that his car?" asked Perkins pointing to the Nissan parked in the spot in front of the townhouse.

"Yeah, that's his car. Isn't he home? He's usually here in the morning, I see him running sometimes around now."

"No, he doesn't seem to be here but I'm going to try again." Perkins went back to the front door.

"Mr. Kiner are you there?" he said knocking. "This is the police. You've done nothing wrong, we'd just like to have a word with you, if that's ok." There was no answer, so the detective went around to the back of the house. The gate to the small yard was unlatched, so he went into the yard and crossed over to the glass door at the back of the house. Peering through the door he could see Kevin lying on the floor. Broken glass and blood were scattered around the body.

The door wasn't locked, Perkins slid it open. He went over to the body on the floor. There was no breathing, so he checked the pulse for a beat. Nothing. Kevin was dead. He called the station and requested an ambulance.

The detective scanned the room. Besides the furniture the only notable thing in the room was a large fish tank. There were some magazines strewn on the coffee table, not much else. It looked like the man had tripped and fallen backward, hit the corner of the glass as he fell, and opened a fatal wound at the back of his head. There was no sign of a struggle, or if anyone else had been in the room. It appeared the death had been from an unfortunate accident, the victim had tripped and hit his head.

Perkins didn't believe in coincidences. *Two people on the same phone call both turn up dead the same day in separate places is not a fucking coincidence. I just don't know the connection yet, but I will.*

Perkins went around Kevin's house carefully to see if he could find any clues. He confiscated Kevin's phone and marked it as evidence. He also checked the car, there was nothing unusual anywhere.

He went back to the station and continued checking Darcy's phone, including her calls, photos, voice mail messages, and appointments.

CHAPTER 50

SLOAN CAME TO the police station the next day and was shown into the detective's office. Detective Perkins had a barrel chest and thick arms from years of weightlifting. He had been in the army before the Fairfax Police Department, and was now in his mid-forties with two tween daughters and a school-teacher wife. He couldn't afford the DC suburbs on a cop's salary, so they lived further out in the county in Centreville. Perkins liked the peace and quiet when he wasn't working, and he didn't mind the commute. He was sipping on some coffee when Sloan showed up at ten am.

"Good morning, Mr. Malone. Thanks for coming in. Can I get you some coffee?

"That would be great, with a little cream if you have it. I hear cops drink the best coffee."

"No, cops eat the best doughnuts, but our coffee is shit, we're too cheap and we have to pay for it ourselves. Still want some?"

"I guess I'll take my chances, doesn't look like it's killing you," said Sloan unaware of the irony as he sat down across from the desk. The room was a cluttered mess of loose papers and unwashed coffee cups. Perkins found a clean mug, poured a cup for Sloan, and gave it to him.

"Thanks very much, Officer," started Sloan. "So, are there any leads in the case? Any idea who did this?"

"Well," answered Perkins. "I'm not sure we have leads exactly, but we do have a bunch of questions."

"Ok, what kind of questions?" asked Sloan.

"Well, let's see. Do you know a guy named Kevin Kiner? Teaches yoga and does training at Donatta's Gym where your wife goes."

He couldn't admit to the police he knew Kevin had shot Darcy, or that he knew anything at all about Kevin. "No, I don't think so," answered Sloan. "It doesn't seem to ring a bell."

"Well, I don't know how to put this delicately, but there were a lot of calls on your wife's phone to and from him."

"Well, I don't know anything about those."

"Do you know what their relationship was?"

"No," Sloan replied. "I don't know anything about him or any relationship. What are you saying?"

"I'm not saying anything, but there were a lot of calls. So, you also don't know anything about the whereabouts of Mr. Kiner?"

"I told you, I have no idea who he is and what he was doing, so I certainly have no idea where he is. Have you tried calling him?"

"We have, Mr. Malone, except he's dead and he died on the same day that someone shot your wife. Do you know anything about that? Seems like quite a coincidence."

"Excuse me, what?" said Malone with genuine shock in his voice. "What do you mean he's dead?"

"He was found dead at his house, a few miles from here," said the detective, who sensed the sudden hesitation in Sloan's voice. "Are you sure you don't know anything about him?"

"Nothing, officer," responded Sloan. "But I'm just confused and shocked. You tell me my wife was doing something with this guy and now he's dead. What the fuck? What happened to him?"

"He fell over at his house, hit his head on the coffee table and bled to death. Could have been punched or pushed, hard to say at this point," said the detective.

"Do you think there's some connection to Darcy, to this burglar? Could this guy have been the burglar? Or was the burglar at his house too?"

"We're trying to figure that out and were hoping you could shed some light on what happened," replied the detective.

"Are you asking if I had something to do with what happened to this guy? And on the same night my wife got shot? Seems like it must have been a busy night."

"Look, I'm sorry for your loss. But I've got two people who knew each other died on the same night but not in the same place. So far there are no clues, witnesses, or suspects, unless you'd like to suggest one or two."

"How would I know? What are you saying to me? Do I need to get my lawyer?

"Look I'm not saying anything, I'm just asking for your help. Seriously, got any idea what might have happened?"

"I don't know what to tell you. A burglar shot her, like I said before. Maybe that was this guy, or someone working with him. Maybe they decided to come over tonight and someone confronted them, so they shot Darcy and then ran off and got in a fight with each other. Maybe, maybe, maybe. I don't know, you're the cops, you're the guys that are supposed to produce the answers, I'm just the guy with the dead wife. So, I don't mean to be rude, but unless you've got some more questions, I've had enough for one day."

"Ok, sorry," said the detective. "I know it's a tough time, I really don't mean to upset you, it's just that I've got to start piecing this together. Unfortunately, since we now know that your wife might have been in a relationship, I need to ask you for your cell phone."

"My cell phone?" asked Sloan. "Why do you need that? I don't get it, and I don't like it."

"Its standard procedure, this could have been a domestic dispute," the detective replied. "You can hand it over or I can subpoena it, won't take long."

"Ok," Sloan said, glaring as he handed over the phone. "But the next time we talk I'll need to have my lawyer with me." Sloan's mind was racing, he knew there was video tape on the phone of Darcy and Kevin, but he also knew resisting handing over the phone would make him look guilty. There was no easy way out of his predicament.

"No problem, I understand," said Perkins. "Can I also get the access code from you?"

"It's the same as Darcy's, 4, 5, 6, 7, just like mine. We kept it simple in case we needed to access each other's phone. When will I get it back? I feel naked without it."

"Thanks very much, Mr. Malone. We'll try to get it back to you in a day or so, no problem. You can go now, we'll let you know if we need anything else."

"Thanks, I guess," said Sloan as he left the station, his mind racing. Kevin's death was nothing he planned on, and he had no idea what to do. What he felt was deep grief, he had lost Darcy, now mixed with the fear of impending doom.

CHAPTER 51

DETECTIVE PERKINS FOUND THE VIDEOS on Sloan's phone the next day and asked him to come back to the station for more questioning.

Sloan processed the shocking news of Kevin's death and decided *I've got nothing to hide. I know the cops will press me for more info. I just need to keep reminding them I didn't do anything to Darcy. And I really don't know anything about what happened to Kevin. Ok sure, I knew about the affair, and I taped it. But that's all I did. And ok, yeah, I broke into Kevin's house and installed the cameras. But old Kevin isn't around to press charges, is he? So what are they going to do? I've done nothing wrong. I won't even take a lawyer with me, that'll show them I'm innocent. A guilty man would take a lawyer with him, I don't need one.*

With his strategy in mind, Sloan was prepared for the questions when he returned to the police station.

"Good morning Mr. Malone," came a cheery greeting from Detective Perkins. He was behind his desk, and Detective Elmont was sitting in a chair near the window. "Can I get you a cup of the world's worst coffee?"

"No," Sloan replied. "I've had the pleasure of your coffee, so I had mine at home this time. What would you like to know now, what can I help you with?" he said with as much innocence as he could muster.

"Well, I suppose you might have an inkling about what we found on your phone."

"I'm not sure I know what you are talking about Detective."

"I'm talking about the pictures on your phone of your wife and Kevin Kiner having sex. Looks like you know who he is after all," responded the detective.

"Oh right, those pictures," said Sloan, who blushed as he pretended to confess. "Yes, I suppose I do know about those. Kevin is his name you say? I'm not sure I knew his name. Darcy did all that, she set up the pictures. She wanted me to get jealous, she sent me all those directly to my phone."

"Nice. And did it work, did the pictures make you jealous?" asked Perkins.

"Not really," said Sloan. The marriage was over, I knew it, she knew it, we both knew it. It didn't matter to me what she did, I just didn't care anymore. Maybe I even liked being a cuckold, who knows? I didn't really look at that stuff after I saw what it was, it wasn't interesting. But the weird, almost funny thing, is that now I really do care about her. More than anything I'd love to have her here right now, right this second. And I'd work on it, I'd care about, about … her."

"And you don't know anything about what happened to Kiner?

"How would I know?" responded Sloan. "They were having an affair, that's all I know."

"Well, how do you know that, besides the videos on your phone?" said the cop sarcastically.

"Again, Darcy did those and sent them to me," said Sloan. "She was taunting me with her affair. She wanted me to give her a divorce."

"Oh really?" said the cop with even more sarcasm. "Then how come there are no videos on her phone, only yours? Turns out these are from cameras that were hidden at his house that are linked to your phone. It looks like you figured out the two of them were getting it on, and you decided to take some pictures, like a real PI. Happens a lot when someone finds out their spouse is cheating. And sometimes the husband not only figures it out, but he also takes care of both of them."

"Well, that's not what happened here. I certainly didn't 'take care of them' as you're implying. I didn't take care of anything. Yes, I have pictures of the two of them, there's no law against that. I didn't do anything. My wife is dead, but I didn't kill her."

"I'd like to believe you," said Perkins, "but you already lied to us about knowing Kiner, and it's pretty obvious you planted those cameras in his house, so why should I believe anything else you tell me?"

"Ok, yeah, I have pictures of my cheating wife," said Sloan. "I'm hardly alone in that. But that doesn't mean I did anything else, because I didn't, plain and simple. And if you want more, you're going to have to charge me with a crime. So, is there anything else you'd like to know?"

"Yeah, there is," said the detective with increased agitation. "You can tell me about the video on your phone where the guy kills Kiner."

CHAPTER 52

"WHAT DO YOU MEAN 'where the guy kills Kiner'? stammered Sloan. "What guy? What the hell are you talking about?" Sloan had no idea what the detective was referring to, he had not looked at the camera's recordings since the night of the shooting.

"I'm talking about the video on your phone that shows what happened to Kiner."

"I don't know what video you're talking about," Sloan replied.

"Seriously?" said the detective. "Have you not seen the video on your phone?"

"Seriously," said Sloan. "I haven't looked at those videos for a long time, they bother me. So, I really do not know what you are talking about. Really."

"Ok then, let's take a look, and maybe you can fill in the blanks," said the detective, who went behind his desk to his computer. He clicked on the video and turned his screen so Sloan could see it as he hit Play. The video flicked on, and Sloan could see Kevin facing the camera and talking to a man who had his back to the camera. There was no sound. Kevin looked agitated, and he suddenly took a swing at the man, who pulled away before the punch could land. The man came back with a hard left hook aimed at Kevin's jaw, but Kevin stepped back, tripped, and fell backwards and out of the picture. The man turned to his right and exited the picture.

"Any idea who he might be Mr. Malone?"

"No. No, sir. No idea," Sloan replied. "I seriously wish I could help you, I got no love for this Kevin guy, trust me. But I have no idea who was with him."

"Are you sure, Mr. Malone? You lied to us before, why should I believe you? Maybe it was some guy you paid to go kill your wife's lover?" said the detective trying to gauge Sloan's response.

"Nice theory," said Sloan. "But do you really think I'd pay some guy and then have a video of the murder sitting on my phone? Wouldn't that be pretty stupid?"

"Well Mr. Malone, in my business, people do the stupidest things you can imagine all day long. I wouldn't have a job if there were no stupid people. Criminals are stupid people, and there are plenty of them around."

"Look, I do not know who he is, I wish I did. Maybe it's the husband of another woman Kiner was fucking, did you think about that? I don't know anything about the guy except he was fucking my wife. That's it, that's all I got. So, you got any other surprises for me? And can I have my phone back?"

"Oh, I'm sorry Mr. Malone. We're going to have to keep your phone now, it's evidence in a murder case. I suggest you go buy a new one. And one more thing. Since this is an open investigation, please don't leave town, we may need to ask you some more questions."

"Oh great, thanks for that. Was the perfect addition to my day, I get to go buy a new phone, and I'm grounded," grumbled Sloan as he left.

CHAPTER 53

AFTER SLOAN LEFT THE STATION Detectives Perkins and Elmont continued discussing the case.

"You know Dave," started Elmont. "I don't believe that guy for a second, he knows more than he's telling us."

"I agree," said Perkins. "After all, he started by lying about Kiner."

"Yeah, I know. And of course, the husband is always a suspect, especially when the wife is having an affair, and this guy knows all about it."

"Yup and yup. And I don't know about you, but I don't really believe it's a coincidence when two people having an affair are killed on the same night. So, here's my theory, tell me what you think."

"Ok, go," said Elmont.

"I think he killed his wife," began Perkins, "shot her and tried to make it look like the burglar had come back. Pretty lame if you ask me."

"Ok, I'm with you, but what about Kiner? Given the time stamp on the video, Kiner was killed while Malone was talking to the EMTs. Malone couldn't have done it."

"Yeah, but what if there was someone else involved? What if Malone paid someone to whack Kiner at the same time he's killing her? After all, he has a great alibi for not being at Kiner's house."

"That would make sense," Elmont replied. "He's got the money, and he's got a motive."

"Yup," said the detective. "Let's get the cell records for Kiner's location around the same time we got the call on Mrs. Malone."

"You got it," said Elmont. "We should be able to get that by tomorrow. I'll put in the request."

CHAPTER 54

TWO DAYS LATER the phone records came back. One name on the phone list stood out to the officers, it was Armando Goya, the man who owned the gun that killed Darcy Malone. They ran a background check on him and there were no convictions, but there was also no work history or other obvious means of support. Goya had no presence on social media, or even a bank account they could find. It was as if he barely existed, except he owned a luxury apartment, an upscale car, a cell phone, and a gun. And he had a Russian girlfriend. The whole picture screamed 'he's a crook' to the officers.

The location data supplied by the cellular carrier showed Armando's phone had been near the Malone home numerous times, including the night of the murder, and later at the Kiner townhouse the same night. Armando had been at the Malone home when

Darcy was shot, and at Kevin's house at the time of his death. Based on the cell records they got a search warrant for Armando's home and cell phone.

He was home when they arrived and knocked on the door.

"Yes officers, what can I do for you now?" asked Armando as he opened the door.

"Sorry to bother you Mr. Goya, but we have a warrant to search your home," said Perkins as he handed the paper to Armando.

"What are you talking about? Because somebody stole my gun and used it?" asked Armando, and there was menace in his voice.

"Unfortunately, Mr. Goya, there's no proof your gun was stolen, there's just what you and your girl-friend say. We have ballistic evidence it was used in a murder, so we are checking everything, that's our job," continued Perkins. "I'd appreciate it if you'd just sit on the couch and not make any trouble while Detective Elmont and I do some checking of your house. Oh, and I need your cell phone too."

"What do you mean you need my cell phone?" growled Armando.

"I mean I need your cell phone, it's included in the warrant," Perkins replied as he held out his hand for the phone. "It would also be nice if you also gave me the access code, so we don't have to crack it open."

Armando complied and gave him the phone and access code. Once the officers had the phone back at the station and were able to access the contents, it didn't take long to find Armando's search for Kevin Kiner's license plate number.

Based on this, they arrested Armando for Kevin's murder. The video from Sloan's phone was critical evidence as it showed a man who looked like Armando from behind. The man was seen swinging his arms, but it was unclear if he contacted the victim. However, it did show the man leaving the scene while the victim was bleeding to death on the carpet. Based on the video, the phone location records, and Armando's license plate search, Armando was charged with second degree murder.

CHAPTER 55

ARMANDO HIRED Leland Kennedy, a man whose elegant bearing and soft Virginia accent belied his history of representing a rogue's gallery of criminals. Kennedy met in private with the prosecuting District Attorney and offered a tantalizing deal, "proof" of Darcy's murderer in exchange for a reduced charge of manslaughter.

Perkins and Elmont theorized Sloan paid Armando to kill Kevin, but there was never any proof. Armando, however, was convinced Sloan had found his gun and used it to kill Darcy when he found her sleeping with Kevin, then tried to make it look like a burglary. The police reached the same conclusion.

The police never believed Sloan's rendition of events. Sloan insisted Darcy was shot by a burglar who panicked and threw his gun in the bushes. The detectives believed Sloan had stolen the Glock from Armando's parked car and used it to shoot his wife who was having an affair with a young instructor at her gym. They believed Sloan used a 'failed burglary' pretense so he could shoot Darcy. The police did not believe there had ever been a burglar, there was nothing tangible except some broken glass to show a burglar had ever been there.

Now, Armando offered something to change their theory of the crime. It was a glistening gold Cohiba cigar band, and the truth about how he came to find Kevin. Armando told the DA that he found the band after a scuffle with a guy behind the Pancake House last November. "We fired a couple of shots at each other, no one was hurt but I panicked and threw my gun in the dumpster behind the restaurant. I went back a few hours later to get back and it was gone, but I found this band lying next to the dumpster.

"I know these cigars, I used to live in Miami, and I know that not just any schmo is going to be smoking one of these babies, they are like twenty-five bucks a pop. Now I'm thinking something might be going on, like someone was following me, I don't know, but it's a strange place to see a band like that.

So, I see if I can track it down, and sure enough, after I go to a few cigar stores, one of them tells me about this Sloan guy. It really bugged me, and I wanted to see what his game is, so I started hanging out near his house to see if anything's going on.

"That's when I see this guy park in front of the house and go in the back, so I wrote down his tag number. Next thing I know, there's a shot and he comes running back around, jumps in his car and drives off. Nothing else to do, I'm not chasing the guy, so I went home to see if I could figure out who he was. Maybe he stole the cigars from Sloan, I don't know. But the tag search comes up, so I go to his house to see what's what, and if he has my gun, I've had enough.

"You know the rest. I went inside and asked him about the gun. I never touched the guy. I swear to God he just got scared and he tripped and hit his head. I didn't know what else to do, so I left."

Based on his testimony, the detectives and DA agreed it was likely Kevin killed Darcy. They figured his target had actually been Sloan, but something went wrong with their plan. They were never sure how Kevin had ended up with the gun, and the cigar band was an enticing clue that somehow Sloan knew more about it than he admitted. They knew it was possible Sloan had found the gun, and that Darcy had given it to Kevin, but they couldn't prove any of that.

The detectives also knew Sloan could have paid Armando to kill Darcy, but again there was no proof. The case was closed, and the DA agreed to reduce Armando's sentence based on the cigar band evidence. That did little to reduce Armando's anger, he was certain that Sloan had taken the gun and the end result for him was prison time.

Sloan was a broken man. He missed Darcy and regretted every day he had not tried to repair the marriage instead of plotting for its ignoble end. Her smell was still in the bed, and it drifted from her closet. He tossed and turned at night, reaching out for her hand in a way he hadn't in years. He knew himself to be a fool, the silly man that first ignored, then turned away, the most precious thing in his life.

CHAPTER 56

A FEW WEEKS LATER there was a third burglary at the Malone home. This time the burglar made no noise as he entered the house and crept quietly up to the bedroom. Sloan was sound asleep; he never heard a thing as the silenced gun pumped a shot into his chest. On the way out of the room the burglar found a fresh Cohiba next to the bed and put it into his pocket before slipping out of the door.

A few days after that, Armando was in his cell when he smoked a Cuban cigar for the first time in years. It had been delivered to him as proof a job had been fulfilled, and he savored every puff.

ACKNOWLEDGMENTS

Thank you to Chris Shaughness, Daniel Myers, and Deborah Jones for their excellent editing and advice.

ABOUT THE AUTHOR

Kalman Stein is the author of *Fun With Words*. He has been privately writing poetry and prose for decades while also functioning as a national non-profit CEO. He holds a BA and an MBA. Since his retirement, his poetry has been published in journals. *A Fly On The Wall* is his first novella.